The Pale Murphys

by Steven Blackwell

◆ FriesenPress

Suite 300 - 990 Fort St
Victoria, BC, V8V 3K2
Canada

www.friesenpress.com

Copyright © 2016 by Steven Blackwell
First Edition — 2016

Contact the Author: steven.blackwell1010@gmail.com

Cover Concept: Brenda Kolasa | www.VisualResolveGraphics.com

Photography: Soaring Like Eagles Photography
Gus Sigurdson | gubby316@yahoo.ca

Social Media: Santana Friesen, Cheryle Gardiner and Bree Baskin

This book is a work of fiction. Names, characters, places and incidents are the product of the authors' imagination or are used fictitiously. Any resemblance to actual events, locales, or persons, living or deceased, is coincidental or has been approved by the individuals who are recognised within the credentials.

All rights reserved. No part of this publication may be reproduced in any form, or by any means, electronic or mechanical, including photocopying, recording, or any information browsing, storage, or retrieval system, without permission in writing from FriesenPress.

ISBN
978-1-4602-9106-1 (Hardcover)
978-1-4602-9107-8 (Paperback)
978-1-4602-9108-5 (eBook)

1. FICTION, GHOST

Distributed to the trade by The Ingram Book Company

About the Book

In 1904, when Edward Murphy decided to break ground in the quiet township of Clover Springs in preparation for the building of his family home, he had no way of knowing that he would also be digging the foundation upon which a house of horrors would stand. His family would learn soon enough. As the decades passed, and the Murphy family tree dwindled to a single branch—with (perhaps) a little help—it was finally someone else's turn.

For the next thirty-three years, other families and individuals would move into the Murphy House and quickly move out again, like fresh air drawn into its lungs and then expelled, fetid and stale. They would be captivated by the house and its surrounding environs, but standing in the dappled shade of an enormous oak, with the sound of the wind whistling through spruce needles and playing among the elms, its idyllic facade hides a terrible past that refuses to stay buried and forgotten.

When the Sterlings buy the Murphy House they have no way of knowing they are immersing themselves in decades of pain, fear, and anguish, accumulated in the house like silt in a reservoir, full to overflowing.

Will the strength of their family's love and loyalty keep them going when so many others have failed?

Can they even survive the infamous Murphy House?

Only time will tell.

Also by Steven Blackwell
232 BIRCH

The townhouse at 232 Birch was haunted. The boy appeared on more than one occasion and he had, more than likely, shown himself on many more instances than ever witnessed. His energy existed in the house, as well as, the surrounding property and he lived in the spare bedroom, upstairs. The same spare bedroom that would become the nursery for two young infants and each would experience the commanding energy, first hand. After time, the frightening spirit of the little boy, known as "Tookie," was predictable and expected. It was the spirit of the man, who was recognized only three weeks before leaving 232 Birch that resulted in an uneasy and confusing reality. It was apparent that they were there, together, all along. Ghosts do exist. 232 BIRCH confirmed it.

http://paranormalauthorblackwell.weebly.com/

Daisy,

Best Wishes!

Steve Blackwell

Nov 1 16

This one is for you, David and Alicia.

xox

The Pale Murphys

1
Bad News

September 2, 1944

The dry needles and leaves from the seventeen spruce, elm, and oak trees that surrounded the Murphy's property were beginning to turn an array of colours. Some of them had already fallen to the ground and began to cover the poorly landscaped lawn. It was apparent that autumn had arrived early this year and the outside air contained an unfamiliar chill for this particular date. It was rumoured to be an elongated, frigid winter, whether they were ready or not.

Inside, Mr. Charles Murphy stoked the fire in the family room while he smoked his pipe. His wife,

Marion, sat on the wing-backed chesterfield helping their daughter with her nightly flash-card lesson. Mother and daughter shared a smile exuding a powerful and truly loving connection, which resonated throughout the entire living space. As the telephone rang, Marion asked her daughter, Dorothy, to keep practising and walked to the kitchen to answer it.

Six-year-old Dorothy Murphy was just commencing her second year of home schooling and was already showing a great deal of improvement over the previous calendar year. In fact, she was displaying a truly remarkable intellect for a girl her age. She possessed a special gift that went unrecognized by her mother and completely dismissed by her detached father. Dorothy was challenged with a speech impediment that caused her to stutter, and was subsequently excluded from the small town's school curriculum. No one in the slight township of Clover Springs was qualified to coach the six year old, and most professed that Dorothy was far too mentally and physically disabled to be assisted by their limited qualifications. They were wrong. Dorothy was an extremely intelligent little girl. Her tiny, underdeveloped brain contained a supremacy that few had been fortunate enough to witness. Sadly, Dorothy also suffered from the early stages of multiple sclerosis—a horrible, debilitating disease that caused her little body to tire easily and made her struggle with her balance.

At times, she would walk with a limp, dragging her left leg behind her. But Dorothy was a happy, content child who radiated an aura of adoration wherever she went. She was a tremendously attractive little girl, with long blonde hair and a defined pair of dimples. It was clear that she got her looks from her mother.

Marion was so proud of her little girl. Dorothy was the second chance she quite deserved. It didn't matter what Dorothy's many limitations presented, Marion placed her on a pedestal. This angered Charles greatly. He felt, at most times, prominently unaccompanied and very disengaged. He would never physically hurt Dorothy, but on the rare occasions that he would speak to her, his voice would be spiteful and demeaning. Dorothy would steer clear of her father most of the time. She did not want to get in his way and ignite his anger.

The town's local doctor had suggested, two years prior, that Dorothy required a specialist in the big city, more than a two-hour drive away. Marion Murphy was in total agreement, but Charles insisted that Dorothy was fine, and that although she appeared to be developing slower than most children her age, she would eventually heal and share the same capabilities as other little girls in her age group. Mrs. Murphy knew that this was not possible, but feared a disagreement with her husband, as he had a fuming temperament when provoked. He finally decided that Dorothy was to dodge the general public as much as possible, escaping any embarrassment that was caused by the ignorant and uneducated town's folk. Her seclusion only added to her many challenges and offered the young girl a limited lifestyle, with no choices of her own.

Charles was a hardworking man, proud and stubborn. He was a hulk of a human being, standing six foot six and weighing in at 295 pounds. With his noticeable hunch though, he slumped to a couple of inches shorter. His eyes were dark and barely managed to open fully, condemned to narrowing by wrinkles and grief. Charles lived in a beaten shirt and brown tattered trousers, rarely wearing shoes (or socks, for that matter). After serving for twenty years in the town's coal mine, he had been badly injured in the collapse of a tunnel in 1929, which killed eight men—a story that made headlines throughout the country. Charles ended up fracturing three of his vertebrae during the unfortunate ordeal, but had been lucky to even escape with his life. As he was unable to carry on with his gainful employment, the Murphy family heavily relied on disability insurance to pay their bills. They struggled to make ends meet and couldn't even fathom affording the medical bills for their daughter's treatments. Charles felt great pressure to provide for his family, but now he was helpless. He felt disconnected from his immediate family—a feeling that escalated steadily and left Charles relying on his fight or flight instincts to stay relevant in his loved one's lives. He would often sit for hours on the bench on the front porch, staring through the trees and glancing occasionally to the sky.

The Murphy family had always been marred by great tragedy. For as long as he could remember, Charles would encounter extreme sadness in and around the house. Ever since the home was constructed in 1904, by his irritated father, most of Charles' memories were filled with calamity and disappointment. As a newly teenage boy, in 1909, Charles had watched with his older brother as their mother died from tuberculosis in the master bedroom upstairs. Then on his nineteenth birthday, in 1915, after his brother had moved away, he had witnessed his beloved father falling down the hand-carved wooden staircase and severely breaking his neck. He was killed instantly. It was at this time in his life that Charles began developing a change of character, and his bitterness became a noticeable inconvenience.

One short year after meeting Marion, in 1918, they married, and Marion gave birth to Jimmy in the summer of 1920. Jimmy was Charles' pride and joy. He gravitated to Jimmy when he was a small boy, and he spent every free moment, away from the mine, hanging out with him and pampering him to an extreme extent—to the point where Marion felt left out a majority of the time. She would cook and clean and tend to Jimmy when he was dependant, but when Charles was at home, Jimmy would be coddled and smothered by him and she was usually not included. When Jimmy was just a young boy, he would spend countless hours playing with his father on the tire swing suspended from the massive oak tree in the far corner of the backyard.

Once Charles had suffered his bad accident, things changed between him and his growing son. Charles grew incredibly angry about his own awful misfortune and spiteful of everyone around him, including his boy—now 15 years old. No one was quite sure why his personality seemed to change. It never came up. As the months went on, Charles would make Jimmy do excessive chores around the house whenever he wasn't involved in his schooling and sporting activities. It would be Charles himself who insisted that his son join the football team, forcefully drilling it into his head, continuously, that winning was imperative. There was no other option.

Jimmy became an impressive, strapping teenager who was pleased to captain his local high school's football team. He was a popular, though average, student and had many close friends. This led to him becoming somewhat rebellious. He was easily pressured, by his peers, into making unpopular and damaging life decisions. The animosity between Jimmy and Charles escalated, and Jimmy grew intimidated by his father. He felt great pressures to succeed and Marion would often become the referee and chief mediator.

Following an impressive championship victory, while Jimmy was 17, he came home late from a party with friends and missed his strict curfew. Upon arriving home, Jimmy was confronted by a visibly inebriated Charles. The drunk man was belligerent and irate over Jimmy's tardiness. After showing uncharacteristic defiance, and trying to explain that he was old enough to make his own decisions, Charles smacked the boy across the face and Jimmy fell to his knees. Charles looked at Jimmy and told him, quite adamantly, that if he missed his curfew again, he would break each and every bone in the boy's body and he would never play football again. The confrontation drove a deep wedge further into their once-stellar relationship, and Jimmy quickly withdrew from his enraged, angry father altogether. Charles chose to make no apologies for his actions, and instead, spited his defiant son for carelessly disobeying his precise, clear, militaristic time-frames. They did not speak to each other for the next four days.

Tragically, on Wednesday of the following week,

Charles found Jimmy hanging from the imposing oak in the back corner of the property. After enduring the destructive argument with his father, on top of whatever else had apparently been bothering him for weeks or maybe even months, he had removed the tire swing, upon which he and his father had played so many times, and replaced it with a hand-braided noose containing exactly thirteen wraps. Jimmy had seemed "not himself" for a long time leading up to the tragic, heart-breaking incident. Marion had suspected that something was wrong, but stayed quiet.

Charles buried his son beside his own mother and father in the family cemetery, also located in the backyard. His personality gradually became almost non-existent, although he seemed much more easily annoyed than usual. He would often be unresponsive to Marion's encouragement and mournful backing, even though it was Marion, herself, who was in clear need of comforting. They had lost their only son, and to make matters worse, the Murphys were now in financial ruin. A mysterious theft had occurred, only two months earlier, with the family's recently inherited fortunes being stolen from their obviously ineffective hiding spot in the basement. The thief was never caught and the investigation had gone cold.

Two years later, on a stifling August evening, Charles arrived home from the town's local watering hole, and in desperation, convinced Marion to conceive once more. Charles longed for another son. Someone to comfort him and take his mind off of Jimmy. Someone to ease the guilt he felt and repair his heart, even though he knew, deep within himself, that it wasn't possible.

The next nine months were difficult for Marion Murphy, but she remained strong. In May of 1938, Dorothy was born. At first, Charles was elated, but as time went on, and he began to discover that Dorothy had challenges, he repeatedly shut himself down once again—slowly, but deliberately, surrendered the raising of his daughter to his wife. At this point, it seemed that nothing would change Charles' motivation.

Marion was contented with these actions. She needed a friend. Someone in her life whom she could rely on and find consolation with. Charles was not that man for her, but she felt it her duty, as a woman, to conform to his wishes. She cooked and did his laundry, but his cold heart just couldn't display any meaningful thankfulness.

Sadness seemed to follow the family throughout their entire time in the small, innocent town of Clover Springs. Their ill-fated misfortunes had quickly led them all into a reclusiveness that caused others to stay clear. Leery, no one in town was willing to befriend the Murphy family and this resulted in an unfair, and perhaps, inaccurate depiction of the entire clan.

The Murphy family, their home, and the surrounding land became known as the *"freak show"* among the local residents. A dreary, dark, and demeaning urban legend was rapidly created. Complaints about the Murphys and their run-down home and property began to roll in to town authorities, who were forced to move the issue up on their priority list. The impressive house itself was randomly vandalized, leaving windows broken and litter strewn about the yard. The Murphy family cowered inside, refusing to take part in any of the drama and hateful activities that occurred around them daily.

And now, to make all of the matters worse, the small town's lot commission had finally decided and petitioned to have the Murphy house bulldozed to the ground. It was a motion proposed due to fact that the house had become an eyesore to neighbours and residents of the small community. The town had plans to turn the property into an enormous family park. Even with Charles' defence, claiming that the house and property had fallen into disrepair because of his accident and lack of monetary funds, the family seemed to be fighting an uphill and losing battle. Town council had been debating and deliberating over the subject for weeks and a decision was expected shortly. Pressure from the local residents had clearly influenced the final decision-making process of the council and hands had been tied.

Marion hung up the phone and re-entered the family room wearing her long, white silk nightgown and slippers. Charles was sitting on his favourite chair, noticeably hunched over, and turned his head, glaring at Marion over the top of his glasses. Dorothy raised her eyes to her mother and noticed a blank, distant, and helpless expression.

"Wh-who was o-o-on the pho-phone, Mommy?" Dorothy asked. The little girl sensed great anxiety and confusion in her mother's aura. After an uncomfortable pause, the little girl shifted her eyes toward her father.

"I think we've actually lost the house," Marion said. She met Charles' steely glare and started to cry uncontrollably. With a purely unemotional demeanour flowing through his body, Charles said nothing. He remained stoic and calm while continuing to puff on his pipe. Dorothy, feeling the tension in the room, turned to meet her father's stare. There was a continual and dead silence for twenty seconds or so, and then Charles slowly stood up and turned away from his wife. Taking four steps toward the blazing fireplace, he reached up and wiped the sweat from his brow. His lips quivered and he slowly turned to Marion.

"No! The hell we have," he stated with firm insistence. Charles headed toward the front door, grabbing his keys off of the side table and slipping on his boots over his bare feet on the way out. "Those bastards will never run me out of my own house! I won't let it happen!"

Marion ran to the door's threshold. "Where are you going Charles?" she exclaimed. "What can you do at this hour?"

Charles ignored Marion's cries and continued to the truck, which was parked midway down the long driveway. After getting into the vehicle, he leaned out and glanced toward Marion. She could see that his eyes were angry, even in the darkness of the front yard.

"Getting supplies!" he yelled as he slammed his door. He reversed onto the main road, his tires spitting up rocks and dirt before catching the pavement and squealing away. Marion watched in despair and sensed a helplessness that convinced her that her desired happiness was lost.

After an overwhelming impression of disappointment, Marion turned swiftly toward her wary, confused daughter and forced a smile.

"Come Dorothy, it's time for some sleep." The little girl, frightened by her father's reaction to the news, made her way upstairs and prepared for bed. Once tucked in, Marion leaned over and tenderly kissed Dorothy on the forehead. She brought the kerosene lantern to the side table beside the closet doors and placed it down. Dorothy needed the light as she fell asleep. It brought her comfort and Marion had repeated the same routine on a nightly basis for the past five years.

"D-do we ha-have to m-m-move, Mommy?" Dorothy asked. "I-I-I don't w-want to m-move, Mom-my. H-How come Daddy said we don't h-have to move b-before he left?"

Marion stared into her daughter's eyes and stroked her long blonde hair with the back of her hand. She fought back tears, keeping them from rolling down her face.

"I don't know sweetheart; I don't know if we will have to move. It will turn out just fine. Sleep now and everything will be better in the morning. I don't think Sally here would be very happy either, if we moved, now would she?" Dorothy smiled and shook her head at her mother, looking at her doll for confirmation.

Marion moved the doll closer to her daughter's chest, smiled, and stood to exit the room. "Goodnight my precious princess. Sweet dreams."

"N-night Mommy, I l-love you." Dorothy had a tear in her eye.

Marion smiled again, turned off the light, and closed the bedroom door tight, retiring to the master bedroom for the evening.

Charles Murphy returned home at about twelve

thirty in the morning. He went straight from his truck to the bench on the front porch and stared into the trees for the next two and a half hours. As the clock struck three, he made his way upstairs to the master bedroom, where he washed his filthy hands and crawled under the covers with his wife. He lay with his eyes open for a few minutes and glared at the ceiling above the bed, muttering to himself. Sometimes an unsound sleeper, Marion woke up and slowly turned over to address her husband.

"Where have you been?" she asked meekly. "It's so late." Charles didn't answer. Marion tried again to get a response. "I'm sorry, Charles. Is there anything that we can do?" Charles didn't move, but stayed turned away from Marion, biting his lip, his eyes wide open. "You have to talk to me Charles … please say something." Finally, after a few painfully awkward seconds, he muttered a response.

"We will be fine," he said. "We will live here forever. This is our home. I will make sure of it. We're not going anywhere."

Marion seemed appeased by his statement, even though she and her husband knew inside that they were living a charade of a truly meaningful relationship. She soon closed her eyes, surrendering to her fatigue, and fell back to sleep.

The Murphy house was quiet and cold. The air was

thick and the window shutters creaked in the early morning breeze. Things would work themselves out. They always had. One way or another.

2
Breaking Point

September 3, 1944

At 4:45 a.m., Marion suddenly woke up to the acrid smell of smoke. She struggled to fully orientate herself from her slumber and turned to Charles, giving him a solid thrust to ensure he awakened.

"Charles!" she exclaimed. "There's smoke! Wake up … Oh God! Wake up!" She continued to shake him and he stirred awake, turning to her.

"What's the matter?" he asked.

"There's lots of smoke!" Marion firmly established. "Something is burning! Can you smell it? It's fire, Charles."

Charles opened his bedside drawer and removed his loaded .44 calibre pistol. They both left the comfort of the blankets and leaped out of bed. Marion ran to the master bedroom's door and twisted the knob, pulling it open. Immediately, she recognized that there was a fire inside her daughter's bedroom. The smoke was seeping through the doorframe and there was a haze throughout the upstairs hallway. Both parents ran down the hall to the helpless girl's location. The door was closed, but now the smoke seemed heavier than only ten seconds earlier and continued to leach through the bottom of the door. Ignoring the searing heat being emitted from inside the room, Marion turned the knob and pushed the door open. The room was filled with dark carcinogenic smoke, which made Marion cough as it wafted out of the entrance and into the hallway. The entire closet area was engulfed in flames, and it had begun encroaching on the surrounding furniture. Marion could just barely see Dorothy through the bitter haze, and screamed her name.

"Dorothy! Speak to me! Oh Dorothy!" Fear coursed through her. Charles grabbed at Marion's arm as she began into the room.

"Wait!" he yelled, "I'll get water!" Charles ran down the hall and into the bathroom. Marion, overcome by fear, ignored her husband's advice, covered her mouth and nose with her hands, and ran into Dorothy's room.

The frantic mother stumbled through the increasing chaos and ran to her daughter's bedside. Dorothy lay motionless and unresponsive on her bed. Her covers were kicked aside, as if she had been in some sort of a struggle. One of her pillows was missing. Marion noticed, in her panicked rage, that the feather-down pillow was lying over by the closet, burning and almost unrecognizable. Marion knelt down beside the bed and put both hands on Dorothy's shoulders.

"Dorothy! Wake up," she pleaded. "Wake up, honey!" Choking on the smoke, Marion looked toward the door. Through the heavy haze that filled the entire room, she watched as the door to the bedroom slammed shut. The sound was terrifying, but now the noise of the intruding flames filled the room. Marion yelled out to her husband.

"Charles! Charles! Help us! ... Charles! ... Oh, for God's sake, please Charles!"

She began coughing and could feel her skin burning from the intense heat. Marion used what strength she had left to grab her unconscious daughter and drag her body from the bed. Marion gently laid on top of Dorothy with a blanket to shelter her, but it was apparent that they needed to get out now or they were not going to make it. Marion dragged Dorothy's limp body across the floor to the closed door. The flames had already been eating away at the frame of the bedroom door and Marion was receiving sever and painful burns to her lower body. Asphyxiated to the point of incompetence, Marion could not reach up to the doorknob. She looked up and screamed out to the best of her ability, but struggled to maintain her flailing consciousness. Her adrenaline exhausted, Marion Murphy made one final, last-ditch effort and prayed for a miracle to occur.

"Help us! Please Charles, we really need help!" Her screams were accompanied by a desperate whimper. They briefly turned into a wailing bellow, and ultimately into a horrific and deafening silence.

The fire continued to spread, fully consuming the little girl's bedroom, and started working its way along the upstairs hallway and into the attic above.

By this time, a neighbour who was woken up by the sound of breaking glass had already called the small town's local volunteer fire department. The dual-engine, eight-man unit was on its way. The neighbourhood's residents began to gather on the streets to watch, but no one rushed to help. Some were sad and sympathetic, but others wished for the old, scary, run-down *freak show* to burn to the ground. Everybody knew the Murphys, but they kept very much to themselves most of the time and people felt uneasy when dealing with the large grumpy father. The fire burnt for just under an hour. Fire fighters arrived from neighbouring counties and the blaze was extinguished before destroying the entire house.

As the sun rose on the Murphys' property, the top section of the house still smoldered. Paramedics and local police had arrived and were carrying out an immediate and thorough investigation. The remains of Dorothy, Marion, and Charles Murphy were removed from the house in body bags and loaded, one by one, into one of the town's ambulances. Onlookers couldn't believe that such a tragic event could have taken place in their quiet, serene community. Most of them were far too young to remember the unfortunate events that had taken place in and around the house so many years ago. The corpses of the Murphy family were taken to the town's mortuary, where they received a mandatory and quite detailed autopsy. The official report was released only one and a half weeks later. Marion and Dorothy Murphy died of asphyxiation, and the patriarch of the family, Charles Murphy, died from a self-inflicted gunshot wound to the head. The story became a top news headline throughout the county.

Authorities were able to contact the only sibling of Charles Murphy to break the news to him. It was his older brother, Peter, who was living on a different continent at the time. Peter Murphy lived alone. Now in his sixties, he was the last surviving Murphy in their immediate family tree. Peter Murphy travelled to Clover Springs and joined the small handful of locals who attended the mass family funeral. He wore a black suit and recognized not one the few patrons who bothered to show up at the burial. Peter stood emotionless as the preacher spoke. He hadn't had much contact with this brother since their father had died in 1915. He'd never had a chance to meet Dorothy, and Marion was so detached from her husband and dedicated to her child that she hadn't attempted to make contact with him for many years. Still, Peter knew that he was the only named beneficiary of the estate. Decisions would have to be made about the house and property. The Murphy family was laid to rest in Clover Springs' small and lonely cemetery.

As Peter Murphy began to leave the sacred graveyard, he was intercepted and approached by a representative of the town's lot commission, who found it necessary to make Peter's day even worse.

"I'm sorry for your loss, Mr. Murphy. You should know that there is an imperative matter that we are required to discuss."

Pain riddled his face and sorrow commanded him, as Peter looked up to glance into the man's eyes. "Can't it wait?" he asked.

"No, I'm afraid not," the man said. "I wouldn't be bothering you if it wasn't important."

"Well ... what is it then?" Peter felt greatly disrespected and demanded an explanation.

The man from the lot commission felt intrusive, but knew it was his duty to proceed and explained the inconvenient interruption.

"Mr. Murphy, as the final and sole surviving member of the family, the Murphy house and property have converted to your possession." Peter stared intensely at the man as he continued. "It's our responsibility to let you know that the town's lot commission has voted for transformation of the property. The house is to be demolished and the land will be converted into a public park, as part of our community's beautification project. Of course, you will be pleasantly and fairly compensated sir. You most certainly don't have to worry about that Mr. Murphy."

Peter raised his eyebrows and addressed the man. "You can't do that," he said in a soft voice. "Nothing will happen until I've had a chance to speak to my lawyer."

"That's fine," the man agreed. "Here is my card. Please contact me tomorrow, in the morning, and we will meet to sign off on the required paperwork. Your attorney is more than welcome to attend, of course. I realize this is short notice, but I'm quite sure that a matter such as this will motivate him to witness."

"That won't be possible," Peter confirmed. "He is more than three thousand miles away, but I will assure you that he will have something to say about this."

The man from the lot commission took a step back, removed his hat, and gave a slight bow to Peter Murphy. "My sincere condolences for the loss of your family, Mr. Murphy. We will talk tomorrow. Take care of yourself; I realize this is a difficult time for you." The man turned and headed toward his car.

Peter was noticeably agitated by the news, but remained stoic and displayed a desire to take this unfortunate opportunity as a means of somehow making amends with his brother. He returned to an awaiting taxi cab and made his way back to the local hotel, so he could make contact with his attorney.

After five failed attempts to contact his lawyer and his office, Peter surrendered and gave up any hope of keeping the property. He knew that the time change separating him and his attorney, along with the immense difficulty in communicating overseas, gave little hope that any actual professional assistance would be available in time.

Peter Murphy readied himself for bed and retired for the evening, eventually falling asleep after contemplating any options that were available to him.

At first light, Peter awoke and cleaned up. Exhausted and defeated, he stumbled downstairs to the hotels café for some breakfast. Once he was back in his room, at 9:00 a.m. exactly, he picked up the phone, contacting the gentleman from the lot commission and preparing himself for the final verdict.

"Good morning Mr. Murphy," the man from the town office said. "We have been expecting your call."

"I wasn't able to get in touch with my attorney," Peter said. "What happens now?" He tilted his head to the floor and gripped the telephone tightly.

After an uncomfortable pause in communication, the man on the other end answered. "Mr. Murphy, I have to admit. There has been an error made by our office and its staffing and we would like to apologize in advance."

"An error? And what does that mean, an error?" Peter asked. "I would like to know exactly what you're talking about. Don't be duping me now, you understand? I think you owe me an explanation, don't you?"

"Mr. Murphy, while preparing the paperwork last night, we found a petition in the file of your brother, Charles." The embarrassed man explained further. "The petitioned document gave the Murphy house and its surrounding property heritage rights. So you see, Mr. Mur—"

"What in the hell are you talking about?" interrupted Peter. "Are you saying what I think you're saying?"

"It appears that the property is protected by the Heritage Conservation Act under section fourteen, subsection two." Peter listened intently as the man on the other end of the phone continued. "It stated that any house built before 1905 had the potential to be included within the county's heritage act. It was so requested in the year of 1908 by your father, Edward Murphy, and approved by town council in 1910." The man sighed. "Mr. Murphy, we are so sorry for your inconveniences."

"What happens now?" Peter asked. He clearly had more spirit in his voice.

The man from the lot commission made the options clear. "As the new executor of the estate, you have quite an easy decision to make. You may decide to sell the property to the town, and as planned, the area will be re-developed into a park, or you must repair the property fully, including landscaping and cleanliness detail. At this point, you may decide to occupy the house or ensure it has a competent tenant residing within it. You will be held accountable for upkeep and property taxes until such time as you decide to sell the house and its land."

"You're right; my choice is easy!" stated Peter firmly. "I choose to take ownership of the house and of the property, have the necessary repairs and maintenance addressed, and rent the property until I make further decisions."

"Very well," the man from the lot commission agreed. "My office will draw up the relevant paperwork and you will need to come downtown, to my office, and sign it. There will be strict supervision conducted by the town to ensure that you are adhering to the stipulations. Should you not be able to meet the proper criteria, the town will appeal to the rights and surely take possession of the land. Do you understand?"

"Yes," confirmed Peter. "I understand. That won't be an issue. I owe this to my family. They did not deserve this fate. I will see you this afternoon to sign the papers. Thank you for your time." Peter hung up the phone and stared at the hotel-room wall in wonderment. This fresh opportunity would surely help him heal.

Once the paperwork was finalized and full possession of ownership was handed over to Peter Murphy, he began calling contractors, securing a local company to repair the top section of the Murphy house. Having been promised insurance funds, he hired a professional landscaper to swiftly detail the huge yard, pruning the many trees and planting colourful flowers. Onlookers throughout the community were stunned that the *freak show* was beginning to look normal and more appealing. Peter Murphy even had a massive, twelve-foot iron-clad fence erected. It surrounded the perimeter of the entire property, and in combination with the stunning beautifications, put a complete discontinuance to the vandalism.

Peter Murphy returned home after the first two weeks and managed the project from the comfort of his own residence. The renovation took two months and the final touches were completed during the first snowfall of the year. Peter also asked to have the bodies of his parents and nephew, Jimmy, re-located to Clover Spring's local town cemetery, to be reunited with his brother and his family. The remains were exhumed later in the week. With the help of the town's council, Peter Murphy was able to mortgage the house, just four weeks later, to a young couple with a 7-year-old child. They moved in on November 16, 1944.

In the following twenty-nine years, the aging Murphy house was occupied by a total of eight different families. The first tenants were forced to leave in 1948, as their daughter, now 11 years of age, began hallucinating and getting violently ill. The town's physicians were unable to diagnose her issues locally, so they relocated to the big city for further specialized treatments. The second, third, and fourth tenants resided for a total of ten years, but all left, sighting that the house was uncomfortable or didn't fit their needs. Many stories of noises and voices from within the house were reported and the *"freak show"*, as it had been dubbed many years earlier, gained a newfangled reputation as the town's haunted house. The fifth family, after disregarding warnings from the locals, took possession of the property three months later, and were forced to move out due to a property inspection, which deemed the house to be unsafe because of asbestos in the basement.

After a year-long renovation, the sixth tenant, a single gentleman in his early 30s, moved in. His name was Jack Mobley and there was something peculiar about him. Locals questioned why a young single male would require such a big house for himself. Why would he need to have four bedrooms? Jack Mobley was creepy and unsettled. In the month of October, 1961, the renter decided to throw a party for a number of the local teenagers in the area. He promoted the gathering as a Halloween party at which you could not only defy your parents but also endure a memorable evening in the township's infamous haunted house. Tragically, this night would not end well. A teenage boy, only 16 years old, was found by his peers, dead in the basement and clutching a big kitchen knife that had been forcefully driven deep into his chest. Police arrived and arrested Jack Mobley, as his initials were written in blood beside the young boy's body and the knife contained his fingerprints. Mr. Mobley feverishly denied the accusations, but was eventually sentenced to sixty years without parole for first-degree murder. The house sat abandoned for another four years after this incident. In a newly arranged agreement with

Peter Murphy, the town saw to the upkeep on the property, and a number of cleaning crews were hired to finely detail the interior on a regular basis. Few of the contractors, though, ever returned for multiple visits.

In 1965, a sixth couple began to rent the house. They would often have their many grandchildren stay over for extended visits. The two seniors stayed and lived their life, seemingly peacefully, for six plus years. In the dreary winter of 1971, the elderly couple was found by family members, lying in their master bed together, deceased. A seventh couple moved into the house in 1971, but they too abandoned the property after only a year, complaining of sounds and an alleged "evil" presence that surrounded the property. Most claims manifested from in the basement, bedrooms, and backyard of the house. By now, everyone in the developing community was aware of the recent tragedies in the house. Few, though, were cognisant of its long and brutal history. Most were stories that a majority believed were fabricated and misinterpreted rumours. The old Murphy house had become a staple of local folklore and people around town believed what they wanted to.

In 1973, Peter Murphy passed away peacefully in his home, of natural causes. He was 93 years old. The town, once again, took possession of the property as it was laid out in Peter Murphy's last will and testament. The house sat abandoned for another three years. During this time, town council once again considered demolishing the house and re-building a new structure. They also considered the park concept once again, but nothing was ever agreed on to a majority and the original house remained intact.

In December of 1976, an official offer to purchase the old Murphy house and its property was presented to the town. A real-estate agent was appointed to show the house and plans were made for a meeting the following week. The prospected buyer was a man in his mid-30s from out of town. He was married and had three children, ranging from the ages of 5 to 14 years old.

Another new year was on the horizon, and hope of a fresh beginning blossomed once more—not only for a young family but also for a flourishing community and a condemned property that had been riddled with misfortune and despair.

3

Peaceful Intentions

December 30, 1976

At half past one in the afternoon, a red Dodge van pulled up to the entrance of the property. It rolled onto the long driveway that made its way up to the side of the house. Through the multitude of trees, and to the right, the driver saw a gentleman sitting still on the front-porch bench. He thought it must be the real-estate agent he was scheduled to meet with that day. He wondered why the man would wait on the porch in the frigid temperatures of late December, but continued on to the side of the house, where he parked and exited the van, followed by a young golden retriever. Only moments after knocking on the worn wooden door, it was thrown open and he was greeted graciously by the smiling real-estate agent, who reached out to shake his hand.

"Mr. Sterling, I presume?" asked the agent. He wore a three-piece suit, complete with a red polka-dot necktie.

"Ah, yes," the man answered, accepting and returning the handshake. "Donald Sterling is the name. It's very nice to meet you sir."

"It's a pleasure to meet you, Mr. Sterling. My name is John Fleming; won't you please come in?"

Donald entered the house and felt an immediate sensation of calmness and security. The air was cold and crisp on this late December afternoon, but the house offered a secure feeling of warmth within. It was musty, and dust covered all the surfaces. He glanced around the space and envisioned his family's many belongings occupying the already fully furnished home. Large white sheets covered most of the fixtures throughout the house, and it quickly became apparent that they were very aged and antique—almost vintage upon first glance.

Mr. Fleming guided Donald to the living room. "Where is your lovely wife, Mr. Sterling? I was expecting her to join you today, and perhaps your children. You mentioned on the telephone that you had three, I believe?

"Yes, that's right," Donald agreed. "They really wanted to be here, but my wife ... well she had a last minute meeting with her publisher in the city last night. It went quite late I guess and she decided to stay back at the hotel with the kids and just rest up today. The children were excited to come along, but I wanted to take a good look at the place without too many distractions, so I asked them to stay behind." He looked down to the dog at his feet. "Just me and this little one today, I'm afraid. Luckily, my wife trusts my judgement. We have talked about this for some time now. She wants a quiet, secluded location to spark her inspiration." Donald smirked. "Oh yeah, and a big kitchen. I wasn't supposed to forget that."

"Oh, I see," the agent responded and grinned. "Let's sit down for a moment, shall we, Mr. Sterling?" He gestured with his hand to one of the large living-room chairs. "I would like to know a little bit about you, and I have a few standard questions that I'm required to ask." He shook his head as if it wasn't going to be a concern. "Then I can give you a tour and you can see what you think of the house. How does that sound?"

"That sounds fine," replied Donald.

As the Sterlings' dog started sniffing around, quickly becoming fascinated by the basement door, the two men walked across the creaky hardwood floor and took seats in the living area, where the agent had a glass of water waiting for Mr. Sterling. Donald brought the glass to his dry lips and glanced toward the front bay window leading out to the front porch. His mind wandered slightly.

"Mr. Fleming? Before we get started, and if you don't mind me asking, why were you sitting on the outside porch as I drove up a few minutes ago?" Donald reached up and adjusted his glasses as they slipped down the bridge of his nose.

After a long, bewildered pause, Mr. Fleming answered, "Uh ... I'm truly sorry, Mr. Sterling, but you must be mistaken. I've been waiting for you in the kitchen the whole time." He stared at Donald with a squint in his right eye, and waited for the uncomfortable moment to pass.

After processing this thought, Donald responded, "Oh, oh yes, yes of course. I am most certainly mistaken and I apologize. I must have been seeing things. Forget that I mentioned it; I was imagining."

Mr. Fleming let out a chuckle. "Yes, well that is possible, indeed. It's quite all right." He changed the subject quickly. "So tell me, Mr. Sterling, what do you do? I would like to know a bit about your family. How long have you and your wife been together? Tell me about your children. I like to get to know my clients. I hope you don't think that I'm being intrusive."

"Not at all," replied Donald. He continued glancing to the window, and the porch beyond. "Well, let's see ... I am a freelance photographer looking for a fresh start and a new canvass to shoot." His expression changed, and as he spoke, he began panning the entire living room area with his eyes. "My wife's name is Barbara. She's a well-known, esteemed author and has four best sellers, so far. You may have heard of her?"

"Wow, that is very impressive," Mr. Fleming approved. "Barbara Sterling? ... No, no I don't believe I recognize the name. I'm not much of a reader mind you."

Donald continued. "We have three children. Our oldest is Richard. He's 14. Then there's Mary. She's 11. And finally we have our youngest, Amanda. She's the baby at 5 years old." Donald sipped on his water again.

The Sterlings' dog, whose attention had been riveted to the basement door for their entire conversation, began to whimper.

Donald glanced toward her. "Misty, stop that! Come here right now! I'm sorry, Mr. Fleming. If you were to ask Barbara, we actually have four children, as Miss Misty here seems to be our newest dependant. She's decent to all of the children though, and I think that they're learning some responsibility along the way, so I guess she's not too much trouble. I'd leave her in the van, but it's pretty cold out there today."

"That's okay," the agent chuckled. "She looks quite young. She's probably just a little inquisitive with her new surroundings. I see this a lot with different kinds of animals as they enter a new space for the first time. I've even seen a pet snake once. It was so stressed out by the move that it tried to consume the family dog whole. It succeeded, from what I understand." He shook his head, realizing that he had digressed. "How old is Misty there? About six months or so?"

"Yes, that's exactly right. She's only six months old," Donald agreed. "Quite the handful at times, that's for sure, but the children like her and she really seems to appreciate the attention. Oh, and the best part? We don't have a snake." The two men chuckled.

"She must be a handful," Mr. Fleming laughed again. "Tell me, Mr. Sterling, what brings you to our quaint little community?"

Donald took a deep breath before answering the question, knowing it was a long story. "Barbara and I have been together for about sixteen years now. We were childhood sweethearts." He smiled as he looked at the real-estate agent. "We have been living in the 'big city' and raising our children, quite contently, for nearly fifteen years now and at this point in our lives, we're ready for a change of pace. My photography business has been fairly lucrative and my wife is very much a free spirit. She doesn't like to be in a rut, as she wants to expand on her experiences and gain as much knowledge as she can. She says it helps her artistic abilities and I tend to agree with her." He paused for a moment and appeared to become a tad emotional. "Life for us has been blissful and satisfying. My family is the most important part of my life, Mr. Fleming. I believe that I would go mad without them."

"Well it seems as if you have it all figured out," Mr. Fleming concluded. "It sounds to me as if this house may very well suit your needs quite nicely."

"That's the plan," Donald grinned widely. "We have some big ideas for our future. Our jobs are quite rewarding, as are our children, and life is pretty grand. At least we think so and I guess that's all that really matters."

"I'm so happy for you, Mr. Sterling," said Mr. Fleming. "I hope that you're thrilled with the house and I'm sure you will be satisfied with our little town." There was a short pause in the conversation and then the agent continued. "Mr. Sterling, before we take a tour of the property, I feel that it is my responsibility to provide you with some information that may very well be a deal breaker."

Donald was intrigued. "Okay, what is it? What do you mean?"

Mr. Fleming stood up from the chair and walked to the front window to peer out.

"Mr. Sterling, over the years, this house has gained a reputation with the locals, one that you may not be too happy with. A teenage boy lost his young life in the basement of this house about twelve years ago. He was brutally murdered. You should know this."

Frowning, and looking alarmed, Donald looked over at the man, who continued to gaze out the window. After pondering the horrific scene in the house's basement for a long moment, he spoke. "That is a truly awful story. I can't even imagine what circumstances would need to take place in order to actually take another person's life." Donald rose from his chair and joined Mr. Fleming at the window. When he continued, he found himself speaking softly. "This is an old house. I would imagine that it has many stories to tell. Some, I'm sure, are not pleasant. Wouldn't you agree, Mr. Fleming?"

The real-estate agent quickly turned to Donald and addressed him, face to face. "The house was constructed in 1904 by a family named Murphy. They mysteriously retired from the premises in the mid-forties, I believe. I don't know any of the details on that. I think there have been numerous owners and renters throughout the years, but really, that's all I know."

After thinking for a moment, Donald responded. "I see … well, surely we cannot live in the past, now can we Mr. Fleming?"

"No, no, I don't believe we can. I suppose that wouldn't be fair to the future." The men stared at each other in a brief moment of silence. "Well," Mr. Fleming said finally, "shall we have a tour?"

"Yes, of course," Donald agreed. "I've been looking forward to this for a while now."

Misty began to bark and ran to the bottom of the main staircase, where she peered up toward the landing above. Her eyes fixated on a central focal point and her tail stood straight up at attention. The two men watched the puppy and seemed delightfully entertained. Her head moved slowly from left to right, as if she was watching something intently.

"Misty, what's the matter with you?" Donald asked. "Get over here, girl."

John laughed. "That's all right Mr. Sterling. I'm thinking that she's trying to tell us something. Perhaps the second floor is as good of place as any to begin." The dog slunk up the stairs. "Maybe your Misty girl can be our tour guide. She seems to know exactly what we need to look at first. Animals have an uncanny ability to stake their claims. Shall we then, Mr. Sterling? Please, after you."

The two men proceeded up the stairs and toured the second floor. Mr. Fleming gave a detailed description of the rooms, ensuring to add value and comfort features to his rehearsed talk track. They first entered into the master bedroom, which was across the landing, at the top of the stairs. The bedroom was spacious and inviting. It contained a large king-sized bed with a massive chestnut headboard. The bedroom didn't have a washroom, which Donald knew that his wife would not like, but the openness of the space would surely compensate for that. The window faced the backyard, which displayed a great number of mature, snow-covered trees. Content so far, the men moved out of the master bedroom and toward the bedroom on the left and down the hall. It was another large room with dual walk-in closets and a view of the south-east side of the property. He imagined his youngest daughter, Amanda, residing here. Misty stayed close to the men and explored the top floor, letting out the odd growl once in a while. Donald and John left the bedroom and walked past the staircase again, toward the full bathroom on the left-hand side of the hallway. The bathroom had a large porcelain bathtub and shower combination, a nice two-sink vanity, and a toilet. Everything was clean and very well maintained. It was quite apparent to Donald Sterling that the second floor had been renovated and updated at some point, as the fixtures, although dated, were not original turn of the century pieces like most of the main floor furnishings. John Fleming then took Donald farther down the hall, where a third bedroom was located on the left. It shared its interior walls with the bathroom, was a bit smaller in size, and felt soothing. The room contained some older furniture and had a window facing west, toward the side driveway.

As the men left the room, John pointed out the access to the attic, which was in a closet in the hall outside the room. He described the attic as enormous, sitting above much of the second floor, and having its own window overlooking the vast front yard. This window could be seen from the street outside, in front of the iron fence. Donald told John that he did not need to see the attic at this time, and they both proceeded to the final bedroom on the right side of the hallway. This was another large room, which faced the enormous backyard and north of the property. Donald stared out the window at the impressive foliage of the yard, and turned to the raised wooden frame of the queen-sized bed. He was sure that his son, Richard, would enjoy this room. It offered some privacy and a creative space for the 14 year old. Content, Donald validated his approval to John Fleming and the two men went back down the staircase to continue with their tour. Misty followed quickly behind with her tail between her legs.

John showed Donald the large living room, where they had been seated a little earlier, and expounded on the comfortable luxuries within the room, pointing out the wood-burning fireplace and well-kept furnishings. He spoke briefly about the front entrance and porch before moving to the kitchen. The kitchen displayed appliances from the late sixties, but it was quite spacious and more than adequate, with enough room for his wife, Barbara, to prepare meals for the family. The kitchen snuggled up to a dining area that housed an oak table and six wing-back oak dining chairs. On the walls hung many old and somewhat disturbing oil paintings. They all depicted dark, ominous scenes of the sky, with bending trees in the foreground. Donald knew that those would have to come down, should he move forward with the purchase. After departing the dining room, John took Donald down the hall where there was another bathroom and a cozy den. This room would surely be converted into an office for Barbara to write her novels in. It had a huge picture window, facing the backyard, which showcased the beauty of a multi-treed winter wonderland.

"Shall we continue to the basement?" John asked. "It's a large open area. The space can be well utilized, I believe."

"Yes," replied Donald. "Let's do that. I'm excited to see if there is ample space for me to set up my dark room."

They proceeded to the old door at the entrance to the basement. Misty pointed her nose at the door and stared intently at it as she had before. John opened the door and flicked on the light. Immediately upon descending the stairs, Donald felt a powerful sensation rush through both of his legs. Misty stayed at the top and watched the men as they continued down. A draft of cool, damp air met the men as they entered the lower level of the house. Donald could remember being uncomfortable in his own basement while growing up at home with his folks. This basement was still unfinished and contained an area dedicated to older laundry facilities. There was a long room with a chilly cellar, and another large unfinished room, which could easily be converted to a sleeping area. Donald envisioned this room as his dark room though, where he would develop many of the photos that he would take in the upcoming years. There was also an unfinished bathroom, which was filled with tools and useless junk. The basement was dusty and eerily dark, and had a few pieces of older antique furnishings. Most were in disrepair.

Satisfied with the tour, the two men went back up to the main floor, where John Fleming felt compelled to close the deal.

"Well, Mr. Sterling," he said. "What do you think? You're both self-employed. You are only a short distance from the schools. Do you think that this house will suffice? It's important to me that you, your wife, and your children are comfortable here. That's my priority."

Donald stood in the centre of the living room and nodded his head. "Yes, I believe this will be fine. I think my family will be quite happy here. Let's make the deal. I'm sure my wife and children will approve. I can't wait to show everyone their new home. What do we need to do to move forward, Mr. Fleming?"

A huge smile spread across John's face. "That's great, Mr. Sterling, I will draw up the paperwork. Are you available for signatures on Monday?"

"Monday … that's the third right?" Mr. Fleming nodded and Donald continued. "Yes, I'll come by your office at around nine in the morning, if that's all right with you? I'm really excited to make this change. There can't be anything but good things to come out of this."

Mr. Fleming agreed and the two men firmly shook hands. "It looks as if my family and I will bring in this New Year from our hotel room," Donald said. "Come on Misty, it's time to go." He projected a short whistle in the dog's direction.

The two men and the dog left from the side door. As John locked up the house, he looked back inside, through the window in the door, and paused. He felt a presence, as sense that he was being watched by many sets of eyes. Shrugging it off, he closed the door and the two men vacated the property as a new stage of snowfall started to descend on the township of Clover Springs.

4
Welcoming Committee

January 8, 1977

Once the paperwork was signed, the Sterling parents happily registered their three children into the town's local school system and took possession of their new home on the eighth of January. Donald Sterling planned on picking up his wife and children at the hotel around two thirty and bring them to the new house. First though, he stopped at a grocery store to pick up some dinner—their first dinner at their new residence. After paying for his rations, Donald took his bags and headed toward the parking lot. Before he exited the store, he was stopped by an elderly man who sat on a bench at the store's entrance. He held a cane out in front of Donald to block his path. His left eye was squinted shut and he was missing most of his teeth. Donald smelled the nauseating aroma of rotten flesh. The old man lowered his crooked cane and raised his eyebrows as he spoke.

"*You buy the old Murphy house?*" he asked gruffly.

"Excuse me?" Donald asked, caught off guard by the man's questioning.

The decrepit man continued. "*The old Murphy house; did — you — buy — it -?*"

"Yes I did. Just today."

The old man began to laugh hysterically. Donald looked around the store, and uncomfortable, started to inch away from the stranger. "You will excuse me."

"*Wait!*" The man stopped laughing instantly. He looked up into Donald's face with his one open eye and presented him with a toothless grin. "*That place is a 'freak show.' You know that, don't ya?*"

After staring at the man briefly, Donald took offence and asked the senile man a disgruntled question.

"Why would you say that? Maybe you should mind your own business, old man."

The little senior smiled, his eyes displaying only their whites. "*Don't ya know what happened in that house, ya fool?*"

With increasing anger flowing through his body,

Donald answered him. "As a matter of fact, yes ... I do happen to know what happened in that house. I'm well aware that a boy lost his life there, years back. I've already been told." Donald nodded at the old man and began to walk away again.

"*Wait!*" The man stopped Donald in his tracks again. "*That house is cursed! Don't you know about the family that owned that house in the early days?*"

Donald stood like a statue. His attention riveted on the old man's words.

"I don't see how this pertains to me," Donald said. "Now if you will excuse me please." He took a few more steps toward the exit.

"*That house is haunted, fool!*" The man raised his voice. "*The family that used to live there were crazy! All of them! The boy killed himself and the girl was retarded. The woman was homely and the father ... the father killed them all! Blew their heads off, is the rumour. Then he burned the house to the ground before putting a bullet in his own skull!*"

The man gripped his cane tightly and broke out into laughter again. "*Ha, Ha, Ha, Ha, Ha, Ha. You're not too bright now, are you sonny? I guess you'll have to learn the hard way, like the rest of them.*"

Donald Sterling frowned, getting very angry. "I think you are delusional, old man! Now, please excuse me!" Donald walked away, glancing back at the man, who continued his one-eyed stare. Finally, Donald stopped, chuckled, and attempted to get in the last word. "Thanks for the heads up friend. I'll make sure to heed your words and prepare for the worst."

"Don't be a fool!" he screamed. *"You will be next! You — Will — Be — Next — ! Ha, Ha, Ha, Ha, Ha!"*

Everyone in the grocery store focused on Donald Sterling, following him out of the store with their eyes. No one seemed to pay attention to the old local, who was clearly insane as far as Donald could see. Shaken by the time-worn man's antics, Donald returned to the van, put the groceries into the back, and drove to the hotel to pick up his awaiting family. The entire drive he thought of the stranger's words and the anger that had flowed from him, unnoticed by the other patrons in the store.

Donald left the groceries and Misty in the van and ran up to the hotel room. He opened the door and found his family sitting in great anticipation. The room was filled with smiles. Donald grabbed Barbara around the waist and pulled her close to him. The two embraced in a short but sensual kiss, and stood arm in arm while turning and addressing their children.

"Well then, is everybody ready?" The youngest children rushed over to embrace their parents. They were elated by the thought of their new surroundings. Richard though, the eldest child at 14 years of age, didn't join in the festivities. He sprawled out on the bed, watching television, and didn't really seem at all impressed. After gathering their belongings and checking out, the Sterling family all climbed into the van and made their way to their new home.

The Sterlings' crimson vehicle pulled into the lengthy driveway in front of the house. Barbara smiled and looked over to her husband.

"It's perfect," she admitted. "See? Look kids! It's so big. The yard is amazing!"

Donald drove up the long driveway toward the side of the house. While the other members of the family spoke over top of each other, with their affectionate descriptions of the property, Donald couldn't help but turn his head to the right, toward the front-porch area. He felt much internal relief as the shaded porch was unoccupied, containing only an empty bench and two rickety chairs. The van pulled up to the side of the house and the family exited into the cold January elements. They stood and peered into the vast backyard, struck in awe by the snow-covered foliage.

"Look!" yelled Mary, as she pointed to the corner of the yard. "There's a tire swing on that tree! I can't wait for you guys to push me on it! I've always wanted to try a tire swing! I bet you that it's way cool; don't you think guys?"

Richard hopped back and forth to keep warm.

"Well, we're not playing on it right now. It's way too cold out. Let's go inside."

The rest of the family agreed and they stood in queue while their father found the key to open the door. Misty stood back by the van. Her tail was between her legs and her head bowed with apparent intimidation. The door swung open and a rush of cool, musty air washed out of the entrance. The Sterling group entered their new surroundings, called for their dog to come, waited until she did so, and then closed the door behind them.

Donald Sterling stared at the familiar interior he had viewed only days earlier. He was a tall handsome man. Slender and confident, he exuded moxie with each of his actions. He was a good father, supportive and gentle. Madly in love with his wife, Barbara, he reached out to her and they extended their hands to each other.

Barbara was a beautiful and strong woman. She demanded respect from her children, but maintained a heroic demeanour resulting in a respectful relationship with all of the children, most of the time anyway. Barbara looked over to the children.

"Why don't you kids take a look around?"

Donald gave directions as the children all headed to the central staircase, hand-crafted nearly seventy-five years ago.

"Richard, your room is at the top of the stairs and all the way left to the end of the hall." He continued. "Mary dear, you're going to be in the room right beside the bathroom. Amanda, go with your brother and sister sweetheart. Mary, show Dee-Dee her room. It will be the first bedroom, at the top of the stairs."

The three kids made their way up the staircase. The two sisters ran up quick, while Richard slowly followed behind. Richard paused half way up the flight and looked down at his feet for a moment. Turning back to his parents, he lethargically spoke.

"I don't like it here ... just so you know."

"Why would you say that?" asked Barbara, but Richard didn't answer her. He turned back toward the incline and continued up to the second floor, where the girls had already discovered their new sleeping rooms. Donald and Barbara turned to each other with concern on their faces.

"He will be fine," said Barbara. "He just needs a little time so he can get used to everything. I think that I feel pretty comfortable here. He'll come around."

Donald nodded in agreement. "Well, should we go and take a quick look around? Then I'll make some supper. It won't be much, but we can get better organized tomorrow, once our stuff in the moving truck arrives."

Donald wrapped his arms around Barbara and

gave her a long spirited hug, ending with a passionate and sensual kiss. He lowered his hands and squeezed Barbara's buttocks, causing her to jump and shriek. With a guilty and seductive look, she whispered to her husband.

"Hey ... not now." She smiled and tilted her head. "Behave yourself." They headed to the kitchen and began their tour.

Upstairs, little Amanda Sterling sat on her small single bed and stared at her closet, while holding an old doll she found in the room. Amanda was only 6 years old and quite shy for her age. She spoke very well, but not often. She had shoulder-length brown hair, and that day wore a pair of long brown suede pants, and a wool sweater that had been knitted by her grandmother. As she combed the ratted doll's hair with her tiny fingers, something caught Amanda's attention from the corner of her eye. She turned, and across the room by the closet door, she saw a small ball of light appear near the floor. It began moving, very slowly, from its previous location, up and toward the ceiling, brightening in intensity. Amanda sat on the bed and fixated on the anomaly. Her mouth hung open and a slight smile came across her face. She rose off of the bed and stood, never taking her eyes away from the light. The flawlessly circular light was now the size of a bowling ball and it moved toward Amanda, sinking back down to her level. Amanda stood in awe.

"Who are you?" she inquired, as she tilted her head. Amanda lifted both of her arms toward the ball of light and pushed her hands into its brightness. Her hair began to slowly charge with electricity and stand up in all directions. Amanda laughed playfully, enjoying her new form of entertainment. The ball continued to enlarge as Amanda's arms disappeared within it. Then it suddenly disappeared, as a familiar and boisterous voice interrupted the manifestation.

"Amanda? Amanda?" Mary ran to the bedroom door with a tremendous grin. "Amanda, come and look at my room. It's totally cool!"

Amanda continued staring into thin air, her eyes open wide. She wiggled her little nose and reached up to scratch an itch.

"Hey!" Mary was finally able to break her sister's stone concentration. "Come on brat; come with me." Mary ran into the room and grabbed Amanda's hand, leading her out of her room. Amanda followed, in tow of her sister, and looked back into her room, anticipating the large ball of light to reappear and follow them.

Downstairs, Donald and his wife stood in Barbara's brand new office, where she would skilfully write her new adventures.

"I love it!" she exclaimed. Barbara wrapped her

arms around her husband. "Thank you, so much. I knew you would make a good choice. We will be happy here, I think." The two adults left the room with Misty following closely behind, and made their way to the secured basement door.

"I think I can put my darkroom down here," he said. "Let's go check it out." Donald swung the door open and a cool, musty smell escaped from the basement. He flicked on the light and he and his wife carefully climbed down the stairs. Misty stayed at the top and peered down. She had no interest in following her masters. The Sterling couple made it only halfway down the creaky staircase when the light popped and crackled, eventually burning out.

"Damn!" exclaimed Donald. They froze on the stairs in complete darkness. "We need to get us a flashlight." They looked back toward the dog at the top of the stairs. "Misty girl, go and get us a flashlight." Donald looked through the darkness into his wife's eyes and grinned.

"Well," Barbara added, "since the stuff doesn't come until tomorrow morning, I'm going to guess that we don't have a flashlight."

The happy couple smiled at each other and ascended the staircase, back toward the comforting light from above. Donald closed the door to the basement. "I'll fix it up tomorrow. Shall we make some dinner?"

They walked toward the kitchen and Donald stopped suddenly. "Oh," he said, "I guess I had better get the food out of the van. There won't be much of a meal without that."

"Uh, that's a good idea," Barbara nodded and smirked, letting out a playful snicker. She continued getting things started in the kitchen while Donald threw on his coat and boots.

Richard Sterling, the eldest sibling, stood and stared out his bedroom window, which faced toward the west side of the backyard. Richard had a blank, lifeless expression on his face and his greasy hair was long and ungroomed. His gaze was fixated on the large tree in the corner of the yard. Covered in snow, he looked forcefully at the tire swing. He couldn't take his eyes off of it and an anger intensified within his body. Richard would turn 15 years old in a week, and as puberty inevitably forced its way upon him, he became more and more unimpressed and less interested in any sort of festivities.

The two young girls came scampering down the stairs, giggling and skipping through the living room and making their way to the kitchen. Amanda lagged behind her sister for a moment, before the girls finally approached their mother, who was preparing some water to boil.

"Hey, where's Dad?" Mary asked her mother. "Did he go into town or something? I want to tell him about my room. It's so big and has a giant bed and everything."

"He's just went to the van to get some groceries dear," her mother answered. "He should be back in any minute. Why don't you give me a hand?"

"No, he's not Mommy," Amanda corrected her. "He's sitting on the bench outside. I just saw him." She pointed toward the living room.

Barbara Sterling stared at her daughter with narrowed eyes. She immediately walked out of the kitchen and toward the living room to look out the large picture window leading to the porch. Before she was able to confirm her youngest child's assertion, the side door swung open and Donald entered carrying three bags of groceries. Smirking, Barbara looked down at her daughter and tilted her head, stroking her forehead. Amanda's face turned white and she became frightened. She knew what she had seen.

"Silly girl," the loving mother shook her head slightly. Amanda looked up and didn't understand what she meant. Her mother went back to the kitchen to continue with her tasks.

Donald set the bags down on the kitchen counter. "Look honey." He started putting the groceries in the cupboards. "I even picked up some bread and lunch meat to make sandwiches for school." He was so proud that he had remembered. The girls ran into the living room and started playing with the dog. Misty liked fetching her tennis ball and appeared to become more comfortable as the evening progressed. Richard came down from upstairs and walked right past the girls, sitting on the chesterfield with no emotion on his face.

The family eventually sat down for supper around the dining room table and Donald addressed his family.

"Well, what does everybody think?" There was a short silence around the table.

Mary finally spoke up. "I like it. It's so big and totally cool." She peered around the table, looking for approval from her siblings. "Amanda sure has a pretty neat room," the middle child continued. "And I'm the closest to the bathroom too, that's the best part. We'll have so much fun here, don't you think?"

Barbara looked toward Richard, who stared down at his food and scowled with dissatisfaction.

"Amanda, honey," she changed her direction, "do you like our new house?"

Amanda nodded, "Yes Mommy. I like my room. I have a brand new friend too." The family continued eating while listening to Amanda speak.

"And who's your brand new friend Dee-Dee?" Donald asked affectionately, referring to his youngest daughter by her nickname.

Amanda looked up to her father. "She hasn't told me her name yet, Daddy."

The entire Sterling family looked at Amanda and each took their turn chuckling uncomfortably while enjoying their feast. Richard raised his head unexpectedly, and managed a sentence. "Oh look, Amanda has an imaginary friend already. Isn't she lucky?"

"Come on now, Rich," Barbara weighed in. "Leave her alone. I think it's so cute." She looked to Richard. "How about you, son? What do you think?"

Richard looked down again and played with his food. "I think this place sucks. Something is not right here. I think if we stay here long, something bad is going to happen."

"Hey," Donald reprimanded, "watch your language around the supper table, Rich. And what does, 'something is not right here,' mean? What are you referring to?" Donald raised his voice. "You have to give it a chance, son. Don't make your sisters uncomfortable here. It's new and you have to give it a chance." Donald calmed down long enough to change his tone. "I think we will be really happy here. This is a great opportunity for your mother and me." He looked to his wife. "Just give it a chance."

Barbara smiled and glanced over to Richard in an attempt to comfort him.

"You're going to be fine, Rich. School starts tomorrow and you'll meet lots of new friends." She glanced around to all of the kids. "You all will. Your dad has some great projects lined up and I'm more than halfway done my new book. Now finish up, because it's an early night. You start school tomorrow, so I want you all wide awake and ready to learn. New teachers, new friends, new start for everyone."

The following morning the family met in the dining room for breakfast. After a quick bite to eat, the children ran out to the front street to catch their buses for school.

"The moving van should be here shortly," Donald said. "I'll start a fire." He stepped out the front door and walked down the driveway to retrieve the newspaper. Once back inside, he went to the fireplace and arranged the kindling to light a blaze. When he had it going, he sat down and started flipping through the local rag and immediately noticed a photo of the old man he had encountered in the grocery store the day before. The story read that the well-known, long-lasting citizen of the town had died in his sleep. The death was being investigated by local authorities, but natural causes were suspected. The date of his unfortunate demise was three days earlier. Donald stared at the inked words in disbelief. He glanced toward the kitchen where Barbara was washing dishes, but was far too shaken to speak. He looked down at the newspaper again, and then tossed it into the trash can, trying to forget what he had just read.

The moving van came and left. Barbara set up her office and Donald fixed the light in the basement so he could ready his dark room. The kids' first day of school was successful and the Sterling family slowly gained comfort in their new lives and surroundings. But something was wrong. Something that no one was quite able to pinpoint. Everyone felt uneasy and there were many strange sounds throughout the house that could not be explained. The air in the house was thick and cold. Surely this would improve with time and the promise of a mild spring season ahead. No one in the Sterling family, other than Richard, would admit their fears or inquisitive wonderment to each other. There was no real reason to frighten anyone. The new house was just different and it would take some time to get used to. The house itself, however, seemed to adopt a completely dissimilar strategy.

5
Signs

April 16, 1977

The snow surrounding the Sterlings' property had mostly disappeared. Spring was in the air and the oaks and elms around the property began sprouting buds. The last four months or so had been challenging for the Sterlings. The children were adapting to their new schools, but some were having more trouble than others. Mary was a good student, quite astute, and gained friends easily. Mostly, she was noticeably content and happy with her life. Her sister, Amanda, and she would soon share a birthday together, born exactly six years apart from each other to the day.

Amanda was also thriving with her school work. She was quite intelligent and began to speak up more to friends, siblings, and her folks alike. Richard Sterling, on the other hand, was greatly struggling. He found it difficult to find real friends. This affected his self-esteem and seem to draw him into a depression, which made all matters worse. A junior in high school and having just turned 15, Richard was ridiculed by his peers. He was easily bullied and didn't have enough energy to stand up for himself. Richard's schoolmates teased him about living at the *"freak show."* He was asked, frequently, when his father was going to murder his family, referring to old stories they had heard from birth. They told Richard that his house was cursed and that everyone who had lived there had gone crazy. Richard kept his anger inside of him. He would walk away, most times, but bring his miserable attitude home with him. After supper, on a nightly basis, Richard would simply sit in his room, on his bed, with the door closed shut. This concerned his parents greatly. Barbara made it clear to Richard that she and her father would be there for him and things would improve with time.

Early Saturday afternoon, Mary and her sister, Amanda, went out to the immense backyard to play with their dog, Misty. They took turns throwing the tennis ball back and forth to one another as the dog barked and ran in pursuit. The game slowly moved to the far corner of the yard as Amanda missed the ball through her legs and Misty took advantage, running past her to claim her possession. The ball had come to rest near the gigantic trunk of the old oak tree. Misty picked up her ball and stood facing the tree. Her tail stopped its ritualistic wagging and she seemed paralysed, gripping the ball in her mouth for a moment. Then Misty whimpered and dropped the tennis ball at her paws, making a couple of uncomfortable shuddering movements away from the base of the majestic tree. After two consecutive double-takes to the girls, who were watching and waiting for the dog to retrieve the ball and continue the game, Misty slowly walked away. She left the ball and maintained a tiny whimper as she passed by both girls and headed back toward the house.

"Well, I guess that game is over," Mary stated. "What do you want to do now?"

Amanda looked toward the tire swing, still having a skiff of melting snow upon it.

"Let's play on that," she pointed at the aged hanging piece of rubber.

"Okay," Mary agreed. "That sounds totally cool. I get to go first. Come on Amanda, you can push me. Bet you I can go higher than you can."

The two girls giggled and ran over to the swing,

which was suspended by one of the oak's tremendous branches. Mary jumped on the tire and started to spin around, twisting the rope. It creaked as it rubbed back and forth on the piece of burlap that was nailed to the branch, used to prevent excessive friction.

"Push me Amanda," commanded Mary. "I want to go really high."

The girls continued to play as the bright sun grew stronger, relieving the winter-torn property. The girls laughed and took turns amusing one another.

Inside, Barbara Sterling pecked away on her typewriter in her office. Donald was away from the house shooting a weekend wedding on the other side of town. Richard sat on a chair in his room and stared out at the girls on the swing. He loved his sisters and had enjoyed a stellar relationship with them until just lately. He had become reclusive to his family and the outside world. His parents and peers chalked his behaviour up to puberty and nothing more. Richard suffered with increasing anger though. His grades were much lower than expected and his friends were few. Misty, who had entered through the newly installed doggy door in the side door of the house, whimpered her way into Richard's room and walked over to the boy. Richard tilted his head toward the dog and reached out his hand to pet her. Misty seemed to understand Richard's grief. It was as if she were in tune with his emotions.

"What's the matter girl? You don't like it here either, do you?" The dog whined at Richard's touch. "I think the kids at school are right about this place. Something is not right here. I can feel it. You feel it too, don't you girl?" Misty looked up at him, and he smiled slightly before returning his eyes to the window. He watched as his sisters decided to leave the swing by the big tree and return to the house. They were rushing back and Amanda seemed to be in some sort of distress. Mary ran behind her with a concerned look on her face. He looked up toward the tree again and his face grew expressionless. He took his hand away from the dog and perched both arms on the window sill as his eyes grew larger. In a panic, Richard retreated from the window, past Misty, and into the hallway outside his door. He hesitated for a moment and continued down the long hall toward the staircase, and headed down. With a hurried pace, he made his way to the office as the two girls entered by the side door. Amanda was crying. Perhaps she'd had an accident on the tire swing. Maybe it was something more.

Barbara met the three children at the threshold of the office. All three were showing a different form of peril on their faces.

"What's the matter with you?" their mother demanded. She scanned the faces of the three children. Reaching out to embrace and console her youngest child, Amanda. "Jesus, you all look like you've just seen a ghost. What happened?"

The three Sterling children were breathing heavy. Mary began speaking and seemed to rush her words.

"I didn't see it, Mom. She scared me when she screamed. I asked her what was wrong, but she ran back to the house. I don't know what happened." Mary started to cry. "She told me outside, in the yard, but I don't even know what she's talking about."

Amanda interrupted her sister. "There is a man in the tree, Mommy. I saw him. It was a man in the tree. I think he was sleeping, Mommy."

Barbara immediately glanced at Mary for confirmation. Mary's expression served as validation to her ignorance.

"What are you talking about child? There's a man in what tree?" She bent down to Amanda's level and looked her in the eyes. "You know you shouldn't be telling these kind of stories, right Dee- Dee?"

"But I'm not telling stories, Mommy," Amanda clarified. "There was a man in the tree and he didn't look at me. His eyes were closed and he scared me, so I just ran away." The anxiety flowed through the veins of Barbara as she listened to Amanda speak.

Mary interjected. "I didn't see the man, Mom. I don't know what she means."

The distraught mother grew very impatient. "Now

come on, Amanda, you are scaring your sister and brother too. Tell the truth. You did not see a man in the tree, now did you? And how can a man be sleeping in the tree anyway?"

Amanda stood, shaken and scared. She gulped and began to open her mouth to respond to her mother, but before she could utter a word, Richard interjected.

"She's right Mom ... there was a man up in the tree. I saw him too. From the window upstairs. I saw a man as well."

Barbara had a terrified look on her face and it transferred to her speech.

"Wh-what are you talking about?" she asked. "Why are you saying these things?" Barbara blew right past the kids and moved toward the side door. The children followed closely behind, as she pulled the door open, continuing around the side of the house in her slippers. The four of them and the dog, who had followed, stopped with a clear sightline to the tree in question. The tire swing swung gently in the breeze.

Barbara raised her voice. "You see a man, do you? Where the hell is this man? I don't see any man, do you? All of you kids are scaring me and it's not nice! Why are you telling me these things? I want you all to go to your rooms. Wait until your father hears about this. He won't be happy at all."

"It's true, Mom. It's really true. I saw him with my

own eyes. There was a man in the tree. There was no swing. There was a man. He was hanging in the tree," Richard said, defending his assertion.

"Now!" his mother scolded them. "Go to your room, now! I don't want to hear another word!"

Mary still had tears welling from her eyes, "I didn't see him, Mom. I didn't see any man. I don't even know what they are talking about."

Barbara began to weep. "Now, God dammit!" The loving mother had lost her composure and displayed a previously unseen demeanour.

The children all hastily made their way upstairs and into each of their respective rooms. Barbara stood her ground for a long moment, and could feel her heart racing. Eventually, she slowly made her way back to the office to try to continue her project. She stood just inside the door and thought about her kid's words, finding it difficult to believe them.

Still visibly shaken by the encounter with her children, Barbara felt a sudden and immediate sensation in the room with her. The air surrounding her was suddenly electric and she looked around the room. A tremendous feeling of guilt overcame her. She looked toward the typewriter on the desk and started walking toward it. As she got a little closer, she noticed something startling. The sheet of paper that was in the typewriter was in a different position than it was when she'd exited the room only minutes earlier. She pulled out the chair and sat down in front of her desk, keeping her eyes on the paper at all times. Once she was seated, she plainly could see that the piece of paper she had been working on had been replaced by a fresh, new piece. It had been loaded crooked and tabbed to the midpoint of the page. The paper contained some type. Barbara read it to herself in disbelief.

> "As I was going up the stairs
> I saw a man who wasn't there
> He wasn't there again today
> Oh how I wish he would go away."

Barbara held her breath, but not by choice. She hadn't felt this kind of fear at any time in her life. Her eyes continued to glare at the piece of paper ... and then she turned sharply to look around the room, but she was noticeably alone. Or at least she appeared to be alone. Barbara continued to feel like she had a visitor. Her panic grew to the point where she had to stand up quickly and leave the room. She curled up on the chesterfield in the living room, covered herself with a quilt, and kept an intense stare in the direction of the office door.

Donald Sterling arrived home at 4:36 p.m. to see his wife and Misty lying together, sleeping on the sofa.

He leaned over to give his wife a kiss and she awoke suddenly, disoriented. Barbara pushed Donald away and jumped up from the sofa, grabbing his hand and guiding him toward her office.

"What's the matter with you, honey?" asked Donald. "Are you all right? You're acting a little strange, if you don't mind me saying so."

Barbara pushed open the office door and dragged Donald to the typewriter.

"Look!" she exclaimed. She pointed down at the sheet of paper. Donald leaned over and read the brief poem, and then looked up to his wife after finishing it.

"Are you not feeling well, sweetheart?" Donald was quite serious and asked this with obvious concern in his voice. "What are you showing me? You wrote this? What does it mean?"

Paralysed with dread, Barbara managed to answer her husband.

"I didn't write this. I didn't … I didn't do this," she said. "I was writing, Donald … and I left and talked to the kids; then I came back and saw it. It wasn't there before."

Donald grew confused. "What do you mean, it wasn't there before? If you didn't type this, who did?"

Barbara swung her arms around Donald's shoulders and shook him. "I don't know Donald! I didn't write it!" Donald's eyeglasses loosened and slid down his face. He pushed them back up in front of his eyes as his wife panicked. "And the kids," she continued. "The kids are acting strange. They said that they saw a man in the tree outside!"

"The tree outside?" inquired Donald. "Which tree are you talking about?" He began to show signs of distress as his voice altered slightly from shortness of breath. The usually brave husband showed some vulnerability and Barbara noticed, but didn't comment on it.

"The tree in the backyard. With the swing on it. Mary said she didn't see, but Dee-Dee said she saw a man in the tree. Then Richard said he saw the same thing, from upstairs in his bedroom. I'm so scared Donald. Please hold me."

Donald's mouth hung open as he granted his wife's wish. He tried to remain strong and as calm as he could, but his anxiety escalated and fought him every step of the way. He stroked his wife's back and tried to bring her comfort, but Barbara was nearing her snapping point.

"There must be some mistake," he confirmed. "They must have been playing a cruel and unnecessary prank on you."

"No!" Barbara yelled at her husband. "It is no prank. They believe it and I believe in them. Something is wrong with this place, Donald! Something is very seriously wrong. Don't you feel something funny here?"

Donald jumped back from his wife's tone as if they were magnetic opposites, then moved closer to her again, and continued consoling her. He wrapped his arms around her shoulders and kissed her on the forehead.

"Come on Barb. I Love you. Please don't scare me like this. Let's get to the bottom of this right now." Donald walked to the foot of the stairs and yelled his son's name. "Richard! Richard, come down here right now!"

The eldest child lethargically made his way to the top of staircase and looked down at his parents.

"Come down here now, young man! You have some explaining to do."

Richard hung his head and climbed down the staircase. He sat on the sofa and Barbara sat in the armchair across from it. She was still quite upset and it was apparent to Richard that she had been sobbing a great deal.

Donald paced back and forth in front of the fireplace. He looked appropriately disgruntled at the situation and finally stood still, addressing his son.

"What is all this business about a man up in the tree?" Donald's voice increased in volume. "And why the hell are you screwing around with your mother's typewriter? You were told to stay out of Mom's office, and I can see you moping around here, feeling sorry for yourself. Now you're making up stories, scaring everybody? Come on Rich, I'll give you a reason to be sad if you want. I'll be damned if I'm going to sit here and put up with this kind of crap from you! Enough is enough, do you understand?! I've had it with this attitude that you're displaying."

Barbara spoke up hastily. "No, it wasn't him, Donald. It *couldn't* have been Rich! He was with me in the yard when it happened." She began to sob again.

Donald paused for a long moment and calmed down. He looked from his wife to his son, who stared at the ground at his father's feet.

"Why are you playing these games, son? Please Rich, tell me how we can help you. There's no need for this. Let us make things better. What can we do to help you, bud?"

Richard took his time, but eventually looked at his father, who was projecting an excessive amount of intimidation. Still, Richard was bound and determined to set the record straight.

"There was a man in the tree. I'm not lying and I saw it, just like Amanda. She saw him too."

Donald rolled his eyes and Barbara let out a whimper as she buried her head in her hands.

Richard continued. "I have felt very different since

living here in this house. I hear stories at school. Don't you hear the stories? *Everyone* can't be wrong, Dad." He looked over to his mom. "Mom, I know you feel it too. People say that this place was a '*freak show*'. It still is, they say. Bad things happened here. Ask someone who has lived in town for a while. Find out the truth."

Donald stood paralysed as he listened to Richard. He remembered speaking to the old man in the grocery store and the words that he had preached. Perhaps his son was right. Maybe there was more research that was required. Donald calmed his tone and turned to Richard.

"Okay son, you can go upstairs. We will call you when supper is ready and talk about this more later."

"You believe me, don't you, Dad?" Richard asked. "I'm not lying to you. I don't have any reason to lie to you, Dad. Tell me that you believe what I'm telling you."

"Yes son, I believe you. Now please let me speak to your mother."

Richard turned and headed upstairs. He shifted his head slightly while continuing forward, adding one last thing.

"This house is angry. I don't like it here."

The next four hours passed without further drama. The family ate their supper together without confrontation and no one spoke about the unusual events that had transpired earlier. By nine in the evening, the three children had been tucked into their beds for the night. Donald and Barbara sat down on the chesterfield, together with their loyal dog, Misty. They talked about the spooky experiences, in depth, for another hour or so and gained little intelligence on the confusing and alarming matter. Eventually they embraced, turned off the lights, and headed upstairs to bed.

Once at the top of the stairs, the Sterling adults heard a peculiar noise resonating from inside of Amanda's bedroom. They both hesitated and Barbara slowly pushed her head to the door to listen closer. She could hear her daughter. She was still awake, and seemed to be carrying on a conversation with herself.

"My name is Amanda," the little girl said. "But you can call me Dee-Dee." There was a short pause. "It's nice to meet you, Dortie. I sure hope that we can stay friends forever and ever."

6
Instant Karma

July 21, 1977

As the scalding summer of 1977 moved onwards, life for the Sterling family calmed to a comfortable reality. There were, however, some constants that appeared to transform into everyday monotony. Misty was getting bigger, but still pouted and slithered around the house—especially when around the entrance to the basement. She wouldn't dare go down the stairs, not even once. Richard continued to underachieve at school. He remained very distant with his family and would always stare out of his bedroom window, looking directly at the big corner oak tree.

Amanda, now 6 years of age, spent more time in her room than usual. She seemed to find it easy to entertain herself and more often than not, her bedroom door would be closed. Mary Sterling excelled in most of her core school subjects and enjoyed helping out around the house and tending to her little sister when needed, without complaint.

Donald went down to the basement to develop some film from a photo shoot he had just completed. Times were tough for the Sterling family. Money was tight, and Barbara spent less time in her office writing. Her revenue streams from her past projects were slowly drying up and she used writer's block as an excuse. The truth be known, Barbara was afraid and immensely intimidated within the office. Donald noticed this fact, but avoided confrontation with his fragile wife and continued pushing forward as an optimist.

As Donald entered the basement, he felt an unfamiliar and overwhelming sensation of instant claustrophobia—an awareness that he hadn't experienced the whole time he had been in the new house. He stood at the bottom of the staircase and scanned the unfinished, musty, and desolate underground region. Something was different this time. Donald felt the hairs on the back of his neck stand up and he developed goosebumps on his forearms. The basement was littered with old run-down furniture and ripped pieces of carpet, which shielded the cold concrete floor. He made his way to the darkroom and set down his camera bag to begin developing his film. Without warning, the light, out in the main basement area, flickered and Donald turned toward the bulb through the darkroom's curtain folds. All at once, a door slammed shut. Donald jumped up in fear, dropped what he was doing, and briskly walked out into the large room to investigate. When he peered up the aged and rickety staircase to the main floor, he could clearly see that the door to the basement, at the top of the stairs, was closed. He had left it open when he came down. Who would close the door, and why with such force that he'd heard it so clearly from the darkroom? Donald knew that his wife, Barbara, and the girls had gone downtown and weren't expected back for an hour or so. Richard was home, sick. He was supposed to be up in his bedroom resting. Donald rushed up the stairs and opened the door, but there was no one around.

"Hello, who's there?" he called out. "Barb, is that you?" Receiving no response, he looked over to the stairs leading to the second floor and gazed to the upper level. "Richard? Rich, are you there?" It stayed quiet. Misty rested near the fireplace. She looked up at Donald while letting out a yawn. Donald slowly turned toward the basement and went back down to continue his work. This time, he made sure to close the basement door behind him.

Upstairs, Richard Sterling sat up on the edge of his bed and stared out of the window at the thick oak tree. The tire swing remained motionless in the hot summer sun. It was challenging for him to see the swing through the immense foliage of the nearer trees, but he had mastered the perfect sightline. As Richard's young, conflicted mind wandered, he started a conversation with the house, itself.

"Whatever you are … whoever you are … you need to go away. I have been in three fights already this year because of you." Richard walked to the other side of his room. "You are not welcome here. This is our house!" His anger built and he started raising his voice. "Why do you think you can stay here? Stop scaring us. You are really scaring my little sisters, and my mother too! You are scaring my mother!" He banged on his bedroom walls with his fists. "Leave! Leave! I want you to leave! You are making my life horrible! I hate this house! I hate you! *Go to hell!*" He screamed his last command.

Richard returned to the window after his rant. He leaned to the proper angle to look at the tire swing, but this time the tire wasn't there. Richard gazed in awe at the big oak tree in the corner of the yard. There appeared to be a rope hanging from the branch. It swayed back and forth. He rubbed his eyes after turning away and slowly pivoting back. The tire was back in place. He must have been seeing things. His eyes were clearly playing tricks on him. Richard stared out for a few more minutes, then walked over and grabbed his football off of the shelf near the closet. He twirled it around in his hands for a moment, then brought it to his bed, where he lay down to rest. As he attempted to fall asleep, Richard curled up into the fetal position and rocked back and forth. He started to mumble, but his words were unrecognizable.

After an hour had passed, Donald had completed his work and arrived at the top of the basement stairs, as Barbara and the girls were removing shopping bags from the van. Donald met them at the side door and assisted in carrying stuff inside. Barbara brought in the final bag, laid it down on the kitchen counter, and gave her husband a tight hug and loving kiss. The girls sat by the fireplace, in the living room, and rolled the tennis ball back and forth with their dog, Misty.

Donald poked his head around the corner from the kitchen and addressed the family.

"What do say we all go outside and work on the yard for a bit? I need a hand with the lawn and perhaps Mom can work on the garden." He looked up to his wife. "I'm pretty sure there are a few weeds that the girls can help pull for you." Barbara smiled and nodded her head.

"I'll go up and ask Rich if he feels well enough to join us." She began walking to the staircase and looked back to address the awaiting family. "Just for a short time though, I want to start dinner soon and maybe tackle some writing later."

Donald and the girls headed out the side door and into the backyard to begin some chores. The birds were in full song and the heat pounded down on the mainly shaded backyard. Instinctively, little Amanda immediately looked toward the leaves in the big oak tree, to ensure that the man she had seen a few months earlier hadn't returned.

Once at the top of the stairs, Barbara turned toward Richard's room and made her way down the hall. She opened his door and saw that he was still asleep. His body looked restless and uncomfortable.

"Rich?" Barbara called out to her son. "Rich, are you awake?" Richard didn't respond and was only breathing shallowly once every few seconds. Realizing that her boy needed some more rest, Barbara slowly backed out and closed Richard's bedroom door.

As she turned to head back down the hall, Barbara felt agitated and uneasy. As she approached Amanda's room, she heard a noise from within. It sounded to her like a faint and distant voice. The muted voice of a young female. Immediately, Barbara felt chills throughout her body. She pushed her ear to the door and her mouth hung open in fear. The voice was not constant, but clear enough to create a solid tone when it resonated. Barbara could not make out the wording, but knew, all too well, that her youngest was outside, where she'd followed her daddy and her sister to the garden, only a few minutes earlier. Barbara managed a deep breath and wrapped the palm of her hand around the doorknob. Slowly freeing the latch, she unhurriedly opened the door. The dark room was empty and any noises seemed to have quieted. Barbara used the hallway light as a guide and stared around the room for a moment, finally surrendering to the fact that her brain must have been fooling her. As she closed her mouth, Barbara's teeth chattered, her lower jaw vibrating all on its own. Finally she left, closing the door behind her. She turned her head back down the hall, toward Richard's room again and paused. Eventually though, the concerned mother made her way back downstairs and out through the side door to rejoin the rest of her happy family in the late afternoon backyard sunshine.

During supper that evening, Donald was forced to help Richard down to the dinner table. He was still weak and remained quite disengaged. The family ate quietly and everyone seemed to sympathize with Richard's prolonged illness. Barbara decided to open up a conversation with her loved ones and started with her son, trying to find comfort in his hopefully returning good health.

"Richard dear, how are you feeling now?" There was no answer. After a brief moment, Mary and Donald looked up toward their brother. They displayed a level of confusion, but felt compassion for the troubled teen.

"Richard, your mother asked you a question," Donald stated sharply. "What's the matter with you, boy?"

Richard, reacting to his father's questioning, slowly lifted his head. "I don't feel good. I want to go to bed. You know that I don't feel well. Why do you wake me up and make me come down here to eat? I'm not even hungry. I don't need to eat … it's not even important."

The four other family members stared in concern. Donald took a deep breath and looked at his little girls.

"You two can be excused. Go play for a while please."

The girls looked over to their mother, who nodded slightly while she smiled and attempted to make the situation less uncomfortable.

"Go on now, like your father said. Maybe after dinner we can make popcorn and watch some television. Johnny is on at eight o'clock." Barbara looked at her son. "You like watching Johnny, don't you Rich?"

Richard didn't react again and appeared in some sort of pain. He sat hunched over and a boisterous, guttural sound escaped from his mouth.

"I want to go up to bed," he said. "Can I go back to bed, please? You guys don't understand how I feel. If we stay here, it will only get worse."

Donald waited for the girls to leave the room, looked over at his wife, and then addressed his son.

"I'm worried about you, Richard. I sure hope you know that your mother and I love you very dearly. If there is anything that we can do for you, let us know. We are your parents. That's what we are here for. We love you, son."

Barbara felt a tear well up in her left eye. "Things have been crazy around here lately," she said. "Your dad and I are just concerned, that's all. We want you to be cheerful, just like your sisters. We just want you to be happy, Rich; that's all." Barbara got up from her chair, put her hand on her son's shoulder, and leaned over to kiss him on the forehead.

Richard jerked away, as if offended by his mother's attempt at affection.

"I'm not going to tell you again, I need to go to bed," he reiterated. "I really don't feel good, so let me go and lie down before I get sick on the floor."

The parents looked at each other, still greatly concerned for Richard's wellbeing. Donald stood up and dropped his dinner napkin onto his plate.

"Okay son. If you're not well, then go off to bed. We will miss watching Johnny with you," he continued. "I sure hope you feel better in the morning. The weather is going to be stunning and your sisters miss hanging out with their big brother. The sooner you're feeling well, the better."

Richard stood up from the table and immediately left the dining room, moving down the back hallway, and heading upstairs. Donald and Barbara sat back down and reflected on the misery that their son, Richard, was appearing to endure.

Donald looked to his wife. "I thought that you were going to try and write tonight."

"What do you mean?" Barbara asked.

"Well," responded Donald, "if we watch television, you won't be writing and you said that you were going to write tonight, remember? Are you still afraid of going into your office? I don't think there is anything to be afraid of, dear. We really need you to start writing again. I'm having a hard time finding enough work to keep our heads above water."

Barbara was offended, but knew that her husband was dealing with difficult circumstances, and so she simply smiled.

"Well, I will make sure that I write a bit tomorrow, okay? I promise. Let's spend some time with the girls tonight. They're really confused and require our support right now. Please Donald, try and understand."

She could see the empathy on Donald's face as he

agreed. He rose from his chair, pushed his eyeglasses up on his nose, and started to remove the dishes from the table, pausing and leaning over to give Barbara a kiss on her temple. Barbara looked lovingly into her husband's eyes, sensing that everything was going to be just fine and helped him with the clean-up.

That evening, once the popcorn had been consumed and the Sterling family had shared a good laugh from their television programming, they said their good-nights to one another and all headed up to bed. Misty followed closely behind and joined Mary in her room, sharing the bed for the night. Both Barbara and Donald checked on Richard, as he slept soundly, and told him that they loved him before leaving the room and closing the door. The floors of the house squeaked, and unfamiliar, peculiar noises resonated from within the walls, but this seemed to be unnoticed by the tired and restless family of five.

At around one thirty in the morning, Richard Sterling stirred and sat up on the edge of his bed. He stared straight forward with his expression blank as usual, except for his mouth, which drooped open in disgust. He leaned over to grab his football from his bedside table, then stood up and faced the door to the bedroom. With no reaction, Richard urinated where he stood. The warm liquid ran down his legs and created a puddle on the hardwood floor of his room. Richard took a step forward toward the door and stopped once more for a moment before continuing on, like he was sleepwalking. He left his room and walked down the dark cool hallway. The other bedroom doors were all closed as his family slept contently. Richard, holding his football still, went down the staircase and proceeded to walk through the living room, where he stopped and turned his body to the right. He kept moving forward and stood at the open door to the basement below. There was bright light in the lower level, as the boy peered down into the space below. Richard began his descent, one step at a time, and as he got to the midway point of the staircase, the basement door gently closed behind him, latching shut at the frame. All was quiet again, throughout the house, but unbeknownst to the rest of the Sterling family, a brutal horror was taking place just two floors below them.

 At 3:57 that morning, Barbara and Donald slept soundly in their master bedroom. Barbara then began to shiver so uncontrollably that it woke her up. She lay on her back and stared at the ceiling for a minute or two. A jolting, sudden urge swept over her body. She felt greatly compelled to look up, through the lonely darkness, toward the entrance of the bedroom. As she tilted her head forwards, toward the door and through the black darkness, she witnessed the figure of a woman standing in the open doorway. Surprisingly, Barbara was not particularly frightened. She felt comfort resonating from the energy in front of her. Barbara turned to see her husband in a deep sleep, and rotated back to the nearly solid apparition. She stared in disbelief at the illuminated anomaly inside of her room. The energy of the woman was very clear. Barbara noticed that she didn't have any legs or feet. The figure hovered above the ground and shone brightly, surrounded by a glowing and nearly blinding aura. The spirit had an expressionless appearance, but Barbara could clearly see a well-defined pair of eyes and cheekbones, which appeared to shimmer and flow with her long grayish hair. She wore an old white nightgown and began shifting forwards and backwards from the bedroom to the hallway, using the door's threshold as the midway point. Barbara looked toward her husband again. He remained asleep. As she turned back to the light, she pulled off her covers and spun around to sit on the edge of the bed. She could no longer take her eyes off the vision of the woman, who continued looking at Barbara with an emotionless stare. Barbara could tell that the woman wanted her to follow her though, and so she built up her adrenaline to do so.

The glowing woman moved back into the hallway and disappeared out of Barbara's line of sight, moving toward Amanda's bedroom. Fearing that the energy had vanished, Barbara stood up and rushed to the doorway, being very careful not to wake her husband. She dashed toward Amanda's room and noticed, with her peripheral vision, that the apparition was now floating at the bottom of the stairs. Barbara carefully began descending the staircase, and as she did, the energy of the woman in white retreated to the far end of the living room. Barbara watched intently from the bottom of the staircase. Just then, the radiant brightness moved rapidly toward the closed basement door and disappeared right through it. Barbara walked to the door and placed her hand upon the knob. As she turned it, her inner feelings changed, and all of a sudden, she no longer felt secure or comfortable. She felt a shortness of breath as she opened the basement door and immediately noticed that the light was on. This made Barbara's skin crawl. The energy from the woman had disappeared altogether, but she felt strongly that she needed to continue an investigation of the lower level of the house. It was quiet and Barbara still remained stunned by the amazing appearance of the woman's apparition. She had never witnessed something so spectacular in all her life. Her emotions changed with each movement of the descent, fearing that she had been summoned for a precisely sombre purpose.

 Barbara carefully made her way down the squeaky

basement stairs. Nearing the bottom, she scanned the space in all directions. As she looked toward the far corner of the basement, in a slightly dimmed area of the room, she saw her son, Richard, sitting straight up in a chair, with immaculate posture.

"Richard?" Her motherly instincts easily kicked in as she fully descended the stairs. "Rich?"

Barbara crept closer to her son. As her eyes adjusted, she witnessed a terrifying sight that put her in an immediate panic. She screamed at the top of her lungs in horror and disbelief.

There, in front of her, was her son, his eyes rolled back in his head, showing nothing but the whites. He had dried blood coming from his mouth and it was mixed with a white foaming vomit that ran down his cheeks. His hands were cramped up in a ball and shaped as if he had been clutching something tightly. The boy's long hair had turned completely white and stood up in a spike. Barbara looked down to the ground and saw that Richard's football was completely deflated and covered with blood and tooth marks. Barbara instinctively reacted to the frightening discovery.

"Richard?" Her voice raised a full octave during the simple, one-word question. Barbara began to scream again then, and her body began to tremble. Her high-pitched shriek projected itself and resonated throughout the entire house, interrupting the peaceful silence within.

"Richard?! Oh my God, Rich?! Speak to me, son!" She grabbed his shoulders and began to forcefully shake him. Richard sat upright and rigid, but completely unresponsive. "Help!" Barbara bellowed. "Donald! Help! Oh Rich, please wake up ... don't do this to me! Oh God!"

Barbara rushed to the basement stairs, leaving her son behind and saw that Donald had already arrived at the top, confused and troubled by his wife's desperate plea for assistance. The girls were right behind their father as he began down the stairs. He stopped and turned to both of his daughters.

"You girls stay here!" he commanded them, continuing down one creaky stair at a time. "Barb, what's wrong?" he asked, clearly anxious. "Why are you yelling so loud ... what's happened?"

Misty, who was reacting to the ruckus, began to bark uncontrollably and ran around the living room in a circle. The two girls were petrified beyond belief, but still attempted to corral their pet. This proved to be a challenging task. The girls both wailed and grew extremely uncomfortable in the seemingly long period of time that their parents were downstairs, tending to their brother.

Donald Sterling quickly rushed to Richard's side

and Barbara moved behind him and cried hysterically.

"Rich? ... Richard! Answer me boy!" Donald turned back to his wife and yelled, "You need to call an ambulance ... Now!" Barbara took a few steps back and froze. Donald grabbed his son and guided him off the chair and onto the floor. He looked up to his shocked wife. "You have to go now, God dammit!"

Barbara ran up the stairs to the kitchen and picked up the phone, calling for medical assistance. Donald stayed and continued treating his son.

"Jesus Christ, Richard, speak to me!" Tears welled up in his eyes and he shook in fear. Upstairs, the dog still barked loudly, adding to the immediate chaos surrounding the members of the Sterling family. Life, as they knew it, seemed to have transformed in a single, ever so tragic, defining moment in time.

Barbara sat in the living room with Mary and Amanda. They all shook with fright, helpless and terrified. Once the paramedics had arrived and proceeded to the basement, Misty calmed and stopped her racket. Donald remained in the basement while the emergency personal attempted to stabilize Richard. After fifteen minutes or so, Richard was carried up the stairs by the two paramedics. His rigid and seemingly lifeless body was placed on a gurney at the top of the stairs. The entire family consoled each other's punishing grief, crying hysterically, and remaining overwhelmed by their current, sad circumstances. Barbara climbed into the ambulance with her son while Donald and the girls jumped into the van to follow them to the hospital. As they began to pull out of the driveway, Amanda looked toward the front porch. In the large picture window, she gawked at a faint shape of a light illuminating the darkened living space. Amanda made a fist and rubbed her eyes while sadness shrouded her, resulting in more tears of sorrow.

By seven o'clock in the early morning, the Sterling family were exhausted. They gathered in the small waiting room and took turns pacing, expecting news soon. The doctor finally made his way into the room and had a serious and apprehensive look on his face. The Sterlings gathered around, tired and worn out from their tears.

Doctor Collins took a breath, looked at the parents one at a time, and then gave them the update.

"I'm very truly sorry," he said. "Richard appears to be in some sort of catatonic state. He is unresponsive to any testing or commands. We have stabilized his breathing and his heart-rate for now, but we will need to run some more tests. Your son's jaw is broken. We're not completely sure how at this time, but it appears that he was chewing on something fairly solid and inedible."

Barbara buried her head into Donald's chest and the

two girls latched on tightly to their parent's legs. No one spoke. At that point, there didn't seem to be very much to say. The family sobbed and tightened their grip on one another. Their son was in great danger, but it was the cause of the accident that concerned Mr. and Mrs. Sterling the most. It was obvious that an immediate resolution was required, and Donald developed a look of steel in his eyes that promised redemption.

7

Truth and Consequences

August 1, 1977

More than a solid week had passed since Richard's frightening ordeal. The Sterling parents held a constant vigil over their son. Sometimes they would stand together as Mary watched over Amanda back at home. At other times, they would take turns by their son's bedside. The girls had visited their brother as well. The situation was particularly difficult for little Amanda. She found it problematic, coming to terms with her brother's accident.

Richard's condition had not improved. In fact, doctors gave the stern impression that the Sterling son's health was actually worsening. The boy lay flat on his back, with tubes crowding his mouth and nose. An IV ran into his arm, and loud, distracting machinery surrounded his hospital bed. His eyes remained closed and he hadn't moved since being discovered by his mother on that fateful Friday morning. On this particular day, it was Barbara who stood over Richard's bedside. Her face was riddled with guilt and sagging from fatigue. Donald entered the room from the hallway and placed his hand on her lower back.

"Come with me," he advised. Grabbing Barbara's hand, he guided her, reluctantly, out of the room. Once in the hallway, Donald turned his wife to face him and looked her straight in the eyes. "Do you remember what Rich said? It wasn't that long ago. Do you recall?" Barbara shook her head sadly, not sure what he was getting at. "When he said that there was a man in the tree, remember? Amanda saw it too. Rich said that really bad things have happened in our house. He said that people around town have called our house the *'freak show'*. He told me to ask someone. He told us to find out the truth."

Barbara raised her head. "He kept saying that he didn't like it there. He never did ... from the first day that we moved in. He tried to caution us and we just ignored him." Her voice became angry. "He tried to warn us Donald!" Her irritation quickly turned back into despair. "We didn't listen, did we? Why is this happening? This isn't the way that things were supposed to be." Barbara turned away from Donald's gaze and clasped her hands up around her head, facing the white brick walls of the hospital.

"I'm going to find out the truth," Donald assured his wife. "It's time that we find out what's happening in that house … our house. And more importantly, what exactly it was that hurt our son. First thing in the morning, I'm going to look for answers." Donald closed in on Barbara and moved his mouth to her left ear. "We will get through this," he whispered to her. "We are going to be fine. And so will Rich. I promise you."

Barbara wept on Donald's shoulder. "I sure hope you're right … oh God, please be right. I can't lose him Donald. Not now."

The loving parents stayed until visiting hours were over. They called home every couple of hours to check on the girls. Twelve-year-old Mary Sterling was held responsible for babysitting her sister, Amanda. They would wait on the living-room chesterfield, like usual, cold and afraid. Protected only by their dog, they waited in close proximity to the telephone in the kitchen, eager for any update on their brother's horrific condition. They had difficulty comprehending the scary, unfolding ordeal. It had been a wretched summer for the Sterling family. Time seemed to be of the utmost importance in finding a resolution for everyone involved.

By 6:45 the following morning, Barbara had already vacated their bedroom, and Donald had come down from the second floor, searching for her. Still visibly devastated, he walked through the living room, and glanced into the kitchen and dining-room space, but she was not there. After looking through the window in the side door to confirm that the van was still there, Donald went around to Barbara's closed office door. He opened the door and there sat his wife, typing away.

"Good morning sweetheart," he tilted his head, affectionately.

Barbara stopped typing and turned to her husband. She had been crying recently, but the tears had dried on her face.

"I've been up since four o'clock. I just wanted to write because I couldn't sleep. I really don't know what to do." The emotion flowed through Barbara's weakened body. "I was in the kitchen, waiting by the telephone."

"You wanted the hospital to call?" Donald asked gently.

Barbara looked into his eyes, "No," she firmly corrected him, "I *didn't* want the hospital to call. I didn't want the hospital to call at all."

The two embraced in the middle of the room and Donald held his wife's shoulders as he spoke.

"I can make us some breakfast. Go and wake up the girls. We'll all go and visit Rich and then I'm going to go to the library and maybe ask around town. I'm going to find out." Donald paused and squinted his eyes as he glanced to the side, and then back to his wife. "It was very quiet last night, wouldn't you say?" Barbara nodded to him. "Maybe if an evil exists here, it's done what it wanted to do and it's gone." He tried reassuring his wife. "Maybe it's gone, honey."

Barbara grabbed Donald around the waist and looked up to him, then spoke in a somber and pessimistic manner. "Maybe the evil is gone, Donald. And maybe it's not. But there are others who remain here, I think." She took a long breath. "And for the record … I don't think the evil *is* gone."

The family all drove up to the hospital and visited their still unresponsive and dependant family member. Richard Sterling remained in a catatonic state, but had been sedated so that his body could rest. His jaw had been wired shut, broken by the relentless and destructive gnawing of his football down in his basement. The family stood around him and carried on a normal conversation, which included Richard. Although he clearly couldn't respond, they paused when a question or statement was directed at him, in hope.

Donald gave all of his girls a hug and kissed his son on the forehead. Then he left the hospital and drove to the town's library, which still stood on the same plot of land as when it was built in the late 1930s. It had been modernized and restored in 1972 and was one of the town's celebrated facilities. The little town, by this time, had swelled to a population that allowed a certain level of privacy for the Sterling family. The nightmare with their son had not been reported to authorities and was not strewn throughout the newspapers, so Donald was not stared at around town. Once inside the library, he immediately went to the librarian, nestled behind the long front counter, stamping books.

"Excuse me ma'am. Can you please tell me where I can find your archive section? I'm looking for history of the town and its residency."

The haggard old woman tending the counter blew smoke from her cigarette into Donald's face, turned slightly, and pointed to the back corner of the library.

Letting out a disguised cough, Donald nodded and thanked the woman before quickly walking to the shelves that she had referred to. He scanned the dusty shelves and read the spines of the aged books before choosing an armful.

For the next three hours, Donald Sterling discovered a wealth of information from a number of books about the history of the town he and his family now called home. Donald learned of the tragic disaster that took place in the local coal mine in 1929: a collapse that took the lives of eight local men. He read how there were plans to re-zone his property, scheduled in the mid-1940s. He even found out that his house had qualified as a historical site. Donald eventually came upon the final book in the stack. It was covered in thick dust and apparently unread for quite some time. The book was written in the early 1950s and contained the history of most of the residents from that time. Donald flipped through the book's pages and was able to locate his desired information with the help of an index, categorizing physical addresses. He began to read about the house in which he and his precious family lived and loved.

"Residence built circa 1904. Constructed by Edward Murphy ..." "Oh my God!" Donald whispered out loud in the dark and secluded reading nook in the back corner of the library. His eyes widened and he pushed his glasses tight to his face. "He died in the house ... and his wife too, from Tuberculosis." The book didn't describe Edward Murphy's cause of death and the tragic way he had met his demise. Further down, on the same page, he started to read yet another disturbing paragraph.

"1944... Charles Murphy, his wife, Marion, and their six-year-old daughter, Dorothy ..." He carried

on, focusing only on the words that helped solve the eerie mystery. *"Died in the fire ... cause of the fire was unknown. Suspected arson as the root cause ... father, Charles Earl Murphy, alleged to have murdered his entire family by starting a fire and then proceeded to take his own life, by shooting himself in the head."*

Donald felt nausea build up in his throat. The thought that these horrendous events all took place in his own house was severely disturbing and revolting. He grabbed the book that contained the photos of the entire Murphy family and duplicated them on the copying machine before returning the book to the shelf. He then sat alone, for a long period of time, looking at the pictures while in deep thought.

By half past one in the afternoon, Donald wanted to hurry and get back to the hospital to see his son and other family members. He decided to check on one more source for valuable information and validation about the past. He loaded the film slide from the town's old newspaper archives onto the viewer. There he saw the story of the mine collapse once again. There was also a long story that was published in 1943, describing interviews with town folk from the time, all claiming that the house on the corner lot was possessed and evil. He read that the property was referred to as the *"freak show."* On another slide, Donald read about Jack Mobley, the tenant who was alleged to have killed the little boy in the basement of the house during a Halloween party in 1961. There was reference to a mysterious robbery that had taken place at the Murphy's address in the spring of 1936. The entire family's savings had been stolen and the perpetrator never apprehended, or even identified for that matter. Donald felt that this article had very little relevance to his investigation, and sighed. As he grew tired of reading, Donald massaged his temples to release some tension. He pushed his glasses further up onto his nose and flipped to one last slide, which just so happened to be a news article referring to the awful suicide that took place on his property in 1937. He read the short editorial to himself while holding his breath.

"Jimmy Edward Murphy was found in the backyard of his home ... apparent suicide by hanging, in the backyard oak tree. The father, Charles Murphy, confessed to verbal abuse, which may have caused the teen to take his own life. Charles Murphy declined any further comment."

Donald turned off the viewer. He had seen enough, and after cleaning up, he walked back to the corner nook where he had left the books. He grabbed the first book that he had looked at, remembering that he saw some information about the town's cemetery. He flipped his way through the book until he came to the page, pulled out a scrap piece of paper from his pants pocket, and wrote down the address and precise plot descriptions of the Murphy family's final resting places. He folded up the piece of paper and clutched it in the palm of his hand while making a tight fist. Donald exited the library, nodding to the librarian on the way out, and hurried back to the van.

Donald Sterling drove to the far outskirts of town, to the old and overcrowded cemetery. He parked the van and walked through the endless rows of grave markings while studying the piece of paper he'd written on. Near the far corner of the eerie graveyard, Donald stumbled upon the graves he wanted to see. There, in front of him and lined up side by side, were the resting places of the Murphy family. He walked slowly past each of them, pausing to read the marble tombstones aloud.

"Gladys Marie Murphy, 1866 to 1909." Donald worked out the mathematics in his head. "My God, she was only forty-three years old." Coming to the obvious conclusion that Gladys Murphy was, more than likely, the mother of Charles, he moved on to the next plot.

"Edward John Murphy, 1863 to 1915." This was the man who built his family's house. Donald then strolled up to the next grave. "Jimmy Edward Murphy. Born in 1920 … died in 1937. This was the Murphy's teenage son, who committed suicide in the backyard after the verbal dispute with his father. As he walked to the next site, the frustration within his body grew much more prominent and he read the marker, this time to himself.

"*Charles Earl Murphy, born in 1896... died September 3, 1944.*" Donald looked down at the grave marker and spoke directly to it. "You son of a bitch! Are you the one causing so much sadness in my house? Are you the one who hurt my innocent son? Just like you hurt your own family? You're dead, you bastard. Stay dead! Stay away from my family! Do you understand, fucker? Stay away from my family!"

Keeping one eye on the grave of Charles Murphy, Donald continued down the row to the next ungroomed plot of grass. It contained the body of another Murphy member and Donald's emotions changed as he read the tombstone.

"*Marion Elizabeth Murphy, 1898 to 1944.*" Donald spoke up and addressed the grave of Marion Murphy.

"I feel grief for you, Mrs. Murphy." He glanced back to the grave of Charles. "I'm sorry that your son of a bitch husband took your life away, far too soon. You didn't deserve that at all. If you have any contact with him, Marion Murphy, you let him know to stop what he's doing. He can't hurt Richard anymore. He can't harm anyone anymore. You tell him for me." After pausing, he took five more steps to the right and viewed the next monument.

"Dorothy Elaine Murphy. Born in 1938, died on September 3, 1944."

"She was only six years old," he said aloud. He once again looked to the grave of Charles.

"You bastard! Haven't you done enough damage? You caused your son to take his own life and then you killed the rest of your family. You are pure evil, Charles Murphy. And now you think you can come after my son? You think that *my* family can be your next victims?" Donald stepped back to the left, stopping in front of Charles Murphy's resting place. Without any remorse, Donald spat upon the sacred ground that surrounded the remains of the Murphys' patriarch. Taking one last look at all six plots, Donald lowered his head and stalked away, returning to the van and making his way back to the hospital to check on Richard's status and comfort his wife and children. As he drove, Donald developed an infuriating and painful migraine headache, which pounded in his sinuses and ate at his soul. His concentration wavered and he spent the majority of the short drive speaking to himself, swearing often.

Donald Sterling arrived at the hospital and entered the waiting room where his daughter Mary was reading a book and her sister, Amanda, slept across two chairs.

"Dad!" Mary said excitedly. "You're back!" She

ran up to her father and wrapped her arms around his waist.

"Hello sweetheart." The loving father returned the hug. "Where's Mom? Is she in the room with Richard?"

Mary nodded to him and her facial expression changed to one of worry. Donald leaned over and kissed his daughter.

"Wait here, with your sister. I'm going to go see Mom for a bit, okay?"

Donald entered the room in which his son lay motionless. Barbara sat on a stool near the bed, staring at her son, riddled with devastation. Donald came up behind his wife and placed his hands on her shoulders, making her flinch slightly, her thoughts interrupted. She looked up to her husband.

"Hi," she managed a fabricated smile for Donald. "Did you have any luck?"

Donald glanced to his son and didn't answer her question. Barbara, seeing the concern on her husband's face, updated Donald on Richard's condition. She found it very difficult to speak, as he had been inundated with so much negativity lately.

"There's been no change. He just lies there like this, for hours. Hours and days," she said. "He looks so lost and empty." Barbara began to cry again. "Who did this to him, Donald? Who did this to our Richard? Why him? What did he do to deserve this pain?" The saddened mother was internally terrified and this was apparent. Donald too was very frightened. His anxiety was overwhelming and he began to shake slightly, reaching into his pocket to retrieve his prescribed medication. With promise resonating through his answer, he looked directly into her eyes.

"He didn't deserve this, honey. He didn't deserve this at all. But I think I know who did this to him."

Intrigued, but clearly overcome by emotion, Barbara asked, "Who? Who was responsible for this?" Donald walked around to the other side of the hospital bed and faced Barbara. Then he looked down at his son.

"I believe that the father of a family who lived in our house, back in the forties, may still exist there today as an evil and malicious spirit, Barbara. His name is Charles, and I think that he's the one who hurt our Richard."

Barbara developed an instantaneous chill throughout her entire body. "What do you mean?"

Donald explained his findings to his wife. He described the verbal abuse that Charles Murphy had inflicted and assaulted his son with and the consequential tragic suicide that took place in their backyard tree. Barbara sat, stone faced, and listened intently. He went on to educate her about the fire on that fateful night that killed everyone in the family. Donald assured Barbara that it was Charles Murphy himself who had started the fire and murdered his wife and daughter with a handgun before turning it on himself. He also showed her the pictures of the Murphy family, which he had photocopied at the library, one by one.

Barbara was horrified. "Remember what I told you? After Rich got hurt? A spirit woman guided me to the basement; she made me wake up from my sleep and almost magnetically lured me to Rich. This woman, Donald ... this woman I saw ... could it have been this Charles Murphy's wife? Was she trying to warn me ... maybe?" Donald listened attentively, as his wife continued. "And the kids saw a man in the tree, Donald! A man in the tree! You just said that a boy hanged himself in that tree." Barbara paused and took a shallow breath. "How old was the little girl? Oh my God, Donald! Amanda tells me that she has a friend in her room. I've heard her speaking to her. I'm so scared, Donald! What is happening to us?"

Just then, Richard's fingers began to move. They cramped up and deformed, which created claws on both his hands. Donald leaned over his son.

"Rich? Rich! Speak to me, son. We're right here, Richard, and we're not going anywhere."

Richard remained unconscious and completely unresponsive. The parents hopefully monitored their son, but Richard's fingers gradually and eventually relaxed back into their normal position once again.

After another thirty agonizing minutes, and having the doctor perform a thorough examination of Richard, the Sterling family left the hospital for the night and grabbed some food to eat at one of the local cafes. Neither Donald nor Barbara told their girls about their theories. They didn't want to scare them any more than they already were. As they ate, very little was said by anyone.

The family arrived home in the early evening. Donald and Barbara were apprehensive about opening the door. As they entered the house, something was obviously different. It was so very cold in the house. Even though it was a hot summer day outside, the house was quite noticeably frigid. And something else was wrong too. Their dog, Misty, who routinely rushed to the door with her tongue hanging out, was nowhere to be seen. Mary assumed that she must be in the yard and would come back through the doggy door soon, but still took her sister by the hand and went back outside to find her. Donald ignited some kindling in the fireplace and stoked it high to create warmth, as Barbara sat on the love-seat and buried her head in a cushion, clearly in great despair. As her eyes closed from pure exhaustion, a vision of the family dog blurred through her brain. She envisioned more chaos and she was right.

The two girls came back in from outside and called out to their parents.

"Mom, Misty's not outside. Something must be wrong. She never leaves. She never goes away from the backyard." Mary was very distressed.

Donald and Barbara looked at one another with obvious concern.

"Well then, let's go and find her," Barbara said with determination. "Maybe Dad and I will go down and check the basement and you can take your sister and see if Misty is upstairs." Barbara stared deeply into her husband's eyes and Mary and Amanda were noticeably short of breath as they ascended the staircase.

After a thorough and unsuccessful investigation of the basement, the Sterling parents made their way back to the main floor and jumped at Mary's thundering shout.

"Mom! Dad! Hurry, come here! I can hear Misty I think! She's upstairs somewhere; I'm pretty sure!"

Donald and Barbara hurried up the flight of stairs to meet their daughters, who were standing near the washroom. They looked at their daughters and glanced around the immediate area, but Misty was not there.

"Where is she?" Barbara inquired, looking around in every direction. "I don't even see her. Where is she, Mary?"

Mary looked up and answered her mother. "I don't

know where she is, Mom. I can't see her, but I could hear her whine. She sounded like she was in the walls, trying to tell us where she is. Listen!"

The family members spread out to check all of the rooms, but each was unoccupied and didn't produce the Sterlings' dog. The family's loyal golden retriever was nearly full grown. Weighing in at almost seventy pounds, Misty was a big girl, but always playful and kind to the children. It was quite unusual that she'd disappeared.

The group met in the hallway again, where Amanda stood in front of the large linen closet.

"I think Misty's in the closet," she finally decided. "I heard her ... listen." Everyone focused their direct attention on the closet door, waiting for any sign that the dog was inside. They heard a faint whimper and Amanda tugged on her mother's skirt. "See Mommy! Misty's in the closet. I told you she was in there. How did she get in the closet, Mommy? Misty is a real good runner and likes to play games, but when did she learn to open the closet?"

Barbara inched her hand toward the closet door handle and opened it quickly. They immediately ascertained that their dog was not in the closet, and even if she was ... where could she lie down? The closet was full of sheets and pillow cases, blankets, and towels. Confused and frightened, the family stared into the closet as the faint whimper returned. This time it was longer and recognizably louder. Donald walked to the opening of the closet and looked up to the ceiling. Above the closet was the painted wooden access panel to the enormous, attic above. The noise made itself present, once again, and Donald released the ladder and climbed to the top, where he attempted to push the access panel up and to the side, but it would not budge. Some sort of force was preventing the man's strength from granting him access. Donald yelled out, "Misty girl, is that you? Are you up here?"

The rest of the family stood in shock, looking up at him as he continued to try to push the panel aside. The whimper quickly turned into a loud and constant barking. Donald realized that the dog was probably standing on the access panel, so he used more strength and pushed hard on the board. This time the strategy worked as the force of the man's efforts made Misty move away from the panel. Donald pushed the entrance way to the side and climbed to the next rung of the ladder to get a good look up into the attic. His heart started to race and his breaths became deeper. He couldn't believe what he was witnessing.

"Daddy?" Amanda asked. "Is Misty okay? Why is she in the roof, Daddy?"

After confirming that their dog was present and unhurt, Donald's eyes panned the attic three hundred and sixty degrees before looking down at his daughter through the hole in the ceiling.

"Misty is just fine, honey. I'll try and get her down." Donald made eye contact with his wife, whose face had gone pale. He then looked back to the dog, who wagged her tail with contentment that she had been found. He shook his head and couldn't believe that this could possibly have happened. How did his dog make it into the attic? The thoughts that ran through Donald's head, having read about the long history of the house, brought on an uncomfortable fear. He grabbed Misty around the front legs and supported her weight as he gently lowered her into the arms of Barbara.

Barbara placed Misty onto the ground, and everyone stroked the dog and pampered her. It was then that the telephone rang. Barbara's shot a quick glance to her husband and shook uncontrollably as she tried to calm herself down.

"I think that I better go and get that," she announced. Barbara hurried down the long hallway and into the master bedroom, where she hesitated before finally answering the phone by her bedside.

"H-hello?" She was noticeably shaken.

"Hello, Mrs. Sterling?" The voice on the other end was familiar. There was a pause when Barbara didn't respond, and then it spoke up again. "Mrs. Sterling, this is Doctor Collins here at Mercy General Hospital.

I'm afraid that I have some bad news. Not long after you and your family left this afternoon, your son Richard had a change in his condition. I would advise that you and your husband come back to the hospital immediately."

Barbara demanded an instantaneous explanation from Doctor Collins. "What's happened now, doctor? What is this change in condition? I need to know right now. I can't wait to hear the news until I get to the hospital. Please tell me, is my Rich going to be all right?"

"It may be best if we talked in person Mrs. Ster—"

"What happened to Rich? Tell me, damn it!" Barbara shrieked.

"Very well," Doctor Collins surrendered to his empathy. "Richard began to have a seizure and went into cardiac arrest. We were finally able to resuscitate him electronically." The doctor paused. "Your son is no longer just in a catatonic state, Mrs. Sterling. I'm afraid Richard has slipped into a coma. He is still alive, but we have been forced to connect him to a breathing machine. We can feed him intravenously, but you should know that these situations generally do not end well. I strongly advise that you and your husband come to the hospital as soon as possible, Mrs. Sterling. I fear that your son, Richard, may not pull through. I'm not sure what else I can tell you at this time. I'm terribly sorry to deliver such bad news."

8
Confirmation

January 11, 1979

Nearly six months had passed since the unusual and life-changing event took place with Richard. The Sterlings' son was alive, but remained in a comatose state. Machines allowed him to breath and he received an adequate liquid diet intravenously. The daily routine of visiting their son continued, day by day, but there was one ray of positive hope emerging.

Barbara had begun to write again. Early in the morning and after visiting Richard, she would sit in her office and type away, clearly defying the existing energy that lingered around the property. The pre-sales were pouring in for the established author of more than eighteen novels, four of them hugely successful. She used her writing as an escape and it helped keep her mind off of the sadness that surrounded her son. She found a great deal of comfort altering her vivid imagination into interesting and intriguing fictional accounts.

Activity in and around the house had been very quiet since the phone call. The occurrence with Misty seemed to be the last noteworthy experience to date. There were still random peculiar noises that came from the basement, odd clanging for example, but nothing that seemed to cause further panic. The air remained heavy throughout the house and the frozen landscape outside only enhanced the already emotionless atmosphere inside. Regardless, the once-bitten Sterling family remained on high alert.

It had been the first Monday back to school after the Christmas break, and the two tired girls were sleeping soundly upstairs in their beds. By 11:00 p.m., Barbara left her office, content with her progress, and headed up to bed. Her face sagged and her dark eyes drooped from tiredness. She went into Amanda's room and tucked her youngest daughter tightly into her sheets. Brushing the back of her hand against Amanda's forehead, Barbara smiled and kissed her daughter's cheek. She left and closed the door, then continued down the hall to Mary's room. Barbara entered the bedroom and picked up some clothing that was lying on the floor. Mary was fast asleep and seemed content and at peace. Barbara knew that her middle child was quickly turning into a beautiful young woman, and this made her very proud. Barbara moved the hair out of Mary's face and told her that she loved her very much. After leaving her daughter's room, Barbara stopped by the washroom to clean up for bed.

Barbara entered the darkened master bedroom, where her husband lay on his back with his eyes open, staring at the ceiling. Misty slept soundly on the floor at the end of the bed. Barbara quickly undressed and slipped into her silk nightgown before climbing into bed beside her husband. She rolled over and draped her right arm over Donald's chest. He continued gazing straight up and offered little reaction to his wife's obvious affection. Finally, Barbara tugged on Donald's arm.

"I feel like I'm wrapped up in a cocoon," she said, looking sideways at her husband. "I'm trapped and I can't escape. I rip and tear at the walls that suffocate me daily, but I just can't break free." Donald slowly turned his head toward his wife and made direct eye contact with her. "Is this our fault?" she asked. "Is this my fault, Donald?" Barbara became emotional, once again.

"It's not your fault," Donald whispered. "It's not our fault at all. This is Charles Murphy's fault. There was no way for us to know that this was going to happen. I don't know where he is. I don't know why he hasn't tried pulling something lately, but when he does … I'll be ready for that son of a bitch. He can't run us out of our own house. That won't happen." Donald was clearly agitated.

"What can you do, Donald? What are you going to do when you see this Charles Murphy? When Charles Murphy shows himself to you, what are you going to do about it?"

Donald looked at his wife and remained speechless for a moment, and then finally collected his many thoughts and answered her.

"I don't know," he confessed. "I'm afraid that I won't know until it happens."

The two held each other close and attempted to stay warm. Eventually, the entire grief-stricken Sterling family slept.

At 5:48 a.m., the door to the master bedroom slowly opened. It had not been shut tight as Barbara wanted to ensure that she heard her children if they were in any kind of distress. An almost transparent mist entered the room and floated along the bedroom wall by the doorway. The energy actually pulsed like a heartbeat as it moved, pausing like an inch worm between its movements. It continued along the wall, making a ninety degree turn at the room's corner and intensifying in brightness. The exhausted Sterling adults did not stir, as Donald kept snoring away. It drifted in front of the large wooden dresser at the side of the room. While the energy pulsed from a dull to a vibrant glow, a hairbrush slid off of the dresser and crashed hard to the floor. The Sterlings' slumber remained uninterrupted. After another minute, the brightened mist retreated once again, along its original path—back to the corner and along the wall, as if it were trying to be illusive and discreet. It slowly drifted back into the hallway. After about fifteen seconds, the bedroom door slowly closed once again, and it seemed (for an instant) that nothing at all had occurred.

Only six minutes later, the alarm clock in the master bedroom vibrated and rang loudly. Barbara Sterling woke suddenly, and immediately opened her eyes wide. Donald lay quietly, staring at the ceiling through squinted eyes. Barbara leaned over and kissed her husband on the cheek before climbing out of bed, sliding her feet into her slippers. She looked down and noticed that the hairbrush was lying on the shag-carpeted floor. She walked over to it and wrinkled her forehead, wondering how it could have gotten there. As she picked up the brush, she quickly came to the assumption that Donald must have gotten up in the night and knocked it off as he visited the washroom. She simply returned it to the dresser and forgot about it quickly.

Barbara left Donald snoozing and quietly left the bedroom, proceeding across the wide hallway and into the washroom to clean up and relieve herself. By 6:08, Barbara Sterling left the washroom and headed toward Amanda's bedroom to wake her up and help her get ready for school. She pushed open her daughter's bedroom door and flicked on the light.

Barbara looked across the room and let out a horrific scream, which made Misty, who had followed her down the hallway, jump back with fear and turn down the hall with her tail between her legs. Amanda was also startled and sat up in bed quickly, looking at her mother and seeing the apparent terror in her eyes. There, on the bare wall beside the east-facing window, was a graffiti-like mural, written in a blood-red colour. Barbara read it to herself in complete horror.

> "*As I was going up the stairs*
> *I saw a man who wasn't there.*
> *He wasn't there again today*
> *Oh how I wish he would go away."*

The short and frightening poem was clearly written by a child. Barbara looked down and saw her bright red lipstick tube lying on the floor with its lid off. It had been worn down to a dull nub. She had received that lipstick as a gift from Donald at Christmas time, one month earlier, and kept it on top of her bedroom dresser. Before Barbara could react, Donald and Mary had arrived in the doorway. Barbara knew, right away, that the words were familiar.

"Jesus Christ!" exclaimed Donald. "What in the hell is that" He took a step into his daughter's room. Barbara ran to Amanda's bedside, keeping an eye on the words that had been handwritten across the wall. Both Sterling parents were obviously troubled and contemplated how they were going to handle such an inexplicable and uncomfortable situation.

"Holy shit!" exclaimed the concerned father. "I've seen that before. Where have I seen that before, Barb?"

Mary began to get emotional, evidently alarmed by the unwanted wake up call. Her eyes were riveted to the poem that was written on the wall.

Barbara turned away from the lipstick text and answered her husband.

"From the typewriter. Remember? It's the same poem, Donald! It's the same as the poem that was on my typewriter months ago! Remember me showing you? It was the same day that Rich and Dee-Dee said that they saw a man in the tree."

Donald turned to his middle child. "Did you do this, Mary?"

"No Dad. I didn't do it. It wasn't me." She began to cry uncontrollably.

Turning back to Barbara and Amanda sitting on the bed, Donald attempted to regain his wits.

"Mary, go on now and get ready for school please. Your mother and I need to talk to Amanda for a minute."

"Okay Dad. Is Amanda in trouble? How did she do that, Dad? She doesn't know how to write like that. It isn't her writing."

"I know that it's not her writing, Mary … I know that," Donald admitted. "No, Amanda's not in trouble. Now go get ready for school like I asked. We need to talk to your sister, please."

Mary hurried down the hallway and into the washroom. Donald moved farther into Amanda's bedroom and joined his wife and daughter on the edge of the soft bed. Amanda seemed confused and still a touch lethargic as a result of her recent sleep.

Donald grabbed Amanda's tiny hand and wrapped it in his own as he reasoned with her.

"Amanda honey, how did you do this? When did this happen?"

Amanda looked over to her mother and then to the writing on the wall.

"I didn't do it, Daddy," the little girl said. "I'm still sleepy." She clutched her doll tightly.

Even before their daughter had answered the question, both of the parents knew it could not have been her. The text was written sloppy, but Amanda had not yet grasped the proper literary techniques to master such a poem. And it was written higher than her reach would allow. She would have had to drag a chair to the location and then back to the corner of the room when she was finished. The chair did not seem to have been disturbed.

"Did you see who wrote that on your wall, sweetheart?" Barbara asked. "Who did it, honey?"

Amanda shared glances between her mother, father, and the writing on the white bedroom wall.

"No," Amanda shook her head back and forth with confidence. "I didn't see who painted the wall."

Her parents glanced at one another and were confused by their daughter's terminology. "But I know who did it though." She managed a slight smile as she said this.

"Amanda, you just said that you didn't see who did it." Donald tried to understand. "Honey, if you didn't see who did it, how can you possibly know who did it?"

The little girl looked into her father's eyes. "I didn't see it happen, Daddy. I was sleeping. But I still know who did it. I even knew that it was going to happen, but I didn't know when. It was a surprise you know. I wasn't even supposed to tell you."

"Who was it then, Dee-Dee?" asked Barbara. Her voice shook from a combination of fright and the frigid temperature of the house.

Amanda looked over to her mother and answered as if she should have already known the answer.

"It was my friend, Dortie, Mommy. She told me that she was going to do it too. She told me not to tell you and Daddy, because it was a surprise. Dortie is afraid of the man on the stairs. She tells me about him all the time."

The Sterling parents were quite speechless. Uncomfortably, they met each other's eyes and grimaced at their daughter's claims.

"Amanda dear," Barbara pressed her body next to her child, "your friend, Dortie, do you think it's possible that her name might be Dorothy? Did you maybe hear 'Dortie' when she told you her name?" Chills overcame Barbara and her body quivered quite violently, her mouth hanging open as she awaited Amanda's response.

"I don't think so, Mommy. She told me her name was Dortie. She laughs whenever I call her name." Amanda smiled.

"What does Dortie look like, honey?" Donald joined the conversation. He remembered the photo of Dorothy Murphy he had brought back from the library. He walked over to the wall with the writing and stood facing it directly.

Amanda got out of her bed and walked toward her closet doors, where she hesitated for a moment before turning.

"I don't even know what she looks like, Daddy. She only sparkles when she comes. She comes from there." Amanda pointed at the dual closet doors. "Sometimes, when she's scared, she hides in there. Like now, I bet. Dortie is in there right now, because she's scared, just like you and Mommy."

Donald and Barbara looked past their daughter at the white closet doors. Donald hesitated, looking understandably alarmed. He began to step heavily forward, as though his legs were encased in cement shoes, moving toward the closet. Barbara watched in fear and anticipation as Donald inched toward the double doors and slowly reached out his hand to the knob on the left. He wavered briefly again.

Mary, having dressed for school, came back into Amanda's room, interrupting her father's progress and an uncomfortable silence.

"Mom, I'm really hungry for breakfast."

"Here," said Donald, as he turned away from the closet, "I'll make something fast to eat. How about some cereal today, Mary? Even *I* can make a mean cereal." Donald tried to lighten the moment, but no one else caught on. He put his arm around Mary's shoulder and guided her toward the stairs. "Come on, let's go get some cereal before the bus comes. Mom can help get your sister ready for school."

Barbara watched, briefly, as her husband and middle child headed downstairs. She then turned back toward the red-lipstick-stained wall once again. Amanda watched her mother intently as she made a fist and placed her head against the wall. Barbara's emotions overwhelmed her and the tears started rolling down her face, once again. Witnessing the obvious and traumatic reality that a spiritual entity resided within her youngest daughter's bedroom was merely an emotional appetizer. As her mind began to explore the facts, it didn't take long for Barbara's thoughts to revert back to her son, Richard, and his continually dire circumstances.

While her husband and daughters shared a rushed breakfast in the dining room, Barbara was upstairs, scrubbing the lipstick from Amanda's bedroom wall. She kept her keen and sharp peripheral vision on her daughter's closet doors, expected them to suddenly burst open and expose her daughter's mysterious friend, Dortie.

The Sterling family loaded themselves into the van and Donald drove the tired and shaken girls to school. He then drove to the hospital with Barbara to visit

Richard. The boy would be 16 years old in a few days. He would continue to lie there, a shell of his formal self, kept alive by a series of complex machines. His condition had not changed, and he remained in his comatose state. Barbara and Donald stayed to support him for two hours, and after kissing their son goodbye, made their way back to the house.

In the wooden mailbox was a royalty cheque made out to Barbara Sterling. Her most recent best seller had received a substantial order. She smiled at Donald, who struggled to reciprocate the gesture. Misty wagged her tail and begged at Barbara's side, happy that their adult masters were home. Donald had been contributing adequately as well, but there was very little reason to celebrate. The Sterlings received another piece of mail that had arrived that day. It was a letter from the township. Barbara opened it, and after quickly reading it for herself, summarized the pessimistic document for her husband. Donald watched as Barbara's demeanour changed. She appeared defeated and overcome with guilt.

"It's a collection notice. The folks at the town are saying that our property taxes are in arrears, and if we don't pay what we owe in the next thirty days, we will be required to go to court." She looked up. "This means we would lose the house, doesn't it? We need to go now and pay this bill, Donald."

Donald sighed and knew that the bill had not yet been paid. The Sterlings struggled to stay afloat financially. To make matters worse, Richard's medical bills were quickly adding up, forcing the family to commit their savings to covering the expenses. The Sterling parents knew all too well, without any communication between them, that a decision would soon have to be made regarding their son's care. Barbara lowered her eyes and headed to her office to work. She stopped at the door and turned back to Donald.

"I'm going to write for a while. Is there anything that you need?"

Donald hesitated, looking down at the letter still. He shook his head.

"No, I don't need anything; thank you, dear. I'm going to take a few photographs around the house. If you need me later, I'll be downstairs developing them."

Barbara nodded slightly and opened the office door.

"Barb?" Donald stopped her. "I love you."

Barbara raised her eyes to him and bit her lip, managing a touch of compassion.

"I love you so much," she announced with conviction. Then she turned and went into her office, closing the door behind her. She quickly began typing away.

Donald made sandwiches for his wife and himself. He served Barbara her lunch in the office and then walked around the house, eating while he collected his photography gear. After setting up, Donald immediately went up and into Amanda's room. He set up a tripod at the foot of the bed and slowly walked over to the white closet. Apprehensively, he opened both of the closet doors fully and stared at the clothes hanging within. He walked back to the camera and started snapping off photos of the gaping storage area. He turned the lights off and took even more pictures using his flash. After taking a dozen snapshots of the closet area, Donald had an idea. He unscrewed his camera from the tripod and walked around the entire top floor of the house, snapping off photos in obvious, specific locations like the master bedroom, the linen closet and the attic above, as well as Richard's bedroom. From his son's room, he peered out the window toward the big tree in the corner of the yard. He began to take pictures of the frozen landscape in the backyard, and used his complex camera's zoom features to get close-up shots of the tire swing. After nearly expending two full rolls of film on the second floor, Donald went downstairs and continued to shoot. He took a series of photographs at the bottom of the stairs, looking toward the fireplace and front entrance, including the large picture window facing out to the porch and front yard, which was covered in deep snow. After another twenty-one shots of the kitchen, dining room, and side entrance, Donald took advantage of Barbara's washroom break and took another eight photos inside of her office space. He then walked downstairs into the cold basement, where he used up yet another roll of film. He concentrated on the corner area of the room, where his son had been found catatonic. It was difficult for him to continue, as he envisioned his son in distress.

Retreating to the confines of the secluded dark room, Donald meticulously prepared the developing tank. In complete darkness, he loaded the thirty-five millimetre, black and white film onto the spiral and popped it into the bath, containing water, developer, and chemicals set to twenty degrees Celsius. After following his usual routine, Donald carefully removed the film from the developing bath with his stainless steel tongs and hung them to dry. He exited the basement and returned upstairs, as it was time for him to drive and pick up the girls from school. Donald opened the office door and was going to ask Barbara if she wanted to come along for the ride, but she had fallen asleep in the chair in front of her typewriter. She seemed comfortable, so Donald did not disturb her and quietly closed the office door behind him before leaving the house. Meanwhile, the developing film in the basement prepared a frightening story, which would finally endorse the family's worst fears, and more importantly, lead to a confirmation that would cause a shift in their fortunes.

9
Grinding on the Soul

March 18, 1979

Time was running out for the Sterling family. They were quickly facing a difficult decision, which could cost them their house, their son's life, or (sadly) both. By now, Donald grasped for hope wherever he could find it. He continued to take on photography projects, which along with Barbara's book royalties, helped feed the family. There was nothing extra though. As spring was upon them, the Sterlings began to reconsider their priorities.

Donald drove himself to the county's large central police detachment in the big city. He decided to take the two-hour drive after the local police detachment in Clover Springs had laughed at his grievance and suggested that he take his concerns to a much higher authority. Donald entered the large four-story building, carrying his portfolio folder and wearing his black rubber galoshes. It had been raining hard for three straight days. This only added to the gloom and doom that seemed to face the Sterling family daily. Donald knew that leaving his family for the entire day would be difficult. Barbara was writing but seemed to need her husband close, as she felt more secure with him nearby. The girls were home with their mother on this day, as it was a Sunday. Most importantly though, Donald would be away from Richard. Not knowing how many days were left before Richard could be gone left Donald empty and depressed. Reaching up to adjust his eye glasses, Donald walked up to the reception counter and stated his business.

"My name is Donald Sterling," he announced. "I would like to speak to a detective. Is one available for me to give some information to?"

"And to what is this pertaining," the officer behind the counter asked.

Donald perspired and his anxiety raised to another level. He looked down toward his black leather portfolio and answered him.

"I have some important information about a crime

that took place at my home in Clover Springs. It is imperative that someone hear me out."

"Clover Springs?!" exclaimed the officer. "Why are you not speaking to your local authorities? Shouldn't they be helping you?"

"I was told to come here," Donald raised his voice a few decibels. "They laughed at me, you see. I am hopeful that no one in your office will laugh at me. I don't believe that this is a laughing matter and would appreciate someone hearing me out." The animosity in the grief-stricken father's voice was clear. "This is a matter that you don't want to ignore. I'm not fooling around here, pal. Let me speak to a detective … please!"

The constable scowled at Donald and hesitated for a brief moment. After shifting his eyes around the precinct, he surrendered to his pleas.

"Very well then." He pointed over to the chairs across the room. "Have a seat over there and I'll see if a detective is available." He picked up his telephone and put it to his ear. "What did you say your name was again?"

"Sterling … Donald Sterling." He sat in the indicated chair, shuffling his feet as he watched all the fast-paced activities taking place around him—announcements being made and police officers entering and exiting the precinct. Some processed criminals, and everyone was quite unhappy, or at least, inconvenienced. After about eight minutes, Donald was approached by a tall, burly man with a thick moustache, wearing a hat, a collared shirt, and a thin brown necktie.

"Mr. Sterling?" He extended his hand to Donald.

Donald rose from the chair. "Uh, yes, I'm Donald Sterling. And who are you, may I ask?"

The man put his hand on Donald's lower back and guided him toward his office.

"My name is Detective Grinde. Am I to understand that you have some information about a crime? Here, please, have a seat."

Donald had a seat in front of the detective's desk. Mr. Grinde closed his office door and walked around to the other side of the desk, sitting down in his vinyl swivel chair, and lighting a cigar.

"What can I help you with, Mr. Sterling? What kind of information do you have for me?"

Reaching into his folder, Donald pulled out three of the photographs that he had developed two months earlier.

He slid them across the detective's desk. "Take a look at these. Tell me what you think. I'm very interested to know what you make of these."

The detective was confused. He grabbed the photos and used his fingers to spread them out, side by side, in front of him.

"What, exactly, am I looking at Mr. Sterling?"

"Look!" Donald insisted that the detective ask fewer questions. "These photographs were taken at my house in Clover Springs. Each one of them shows some sort of peculiar anomaly. Some strange figures. Surely you can see what I'm talking about, can't you?"

The police detective studied the black and white photos closely, bringing them up to his face for a closer look, one by one.

"I'm sorry, Mr. Sterling. I don't have the slightest idea what in the hell you're talking about. To me these pictures make absolutely no sense. Am I supposed to know what it is that you're trying to show me?" He stared at Donald, confused, and blew smoke into the air above his head.

Donald snatched away the photograph that the officer was holding and placed it down in front of him.

"I took this picture at the bottom of my staircase. Just two months ago! You can clearly see this man, sitting on the bench on our front porch." He pointed to a shadowy figure that appeared through the big picture window on or around the bench outside. "Do you see this son of a bitch? This bastard killed my son!"

"Whoa ... slow down, Mr. Sterling. What are you talking about?" The detective frowned while taking a sip from his coffee cup.

"And here," Donald rambled on as he grabbed

another photo. "Look here. You can see this bright ball of light in my daughter's bedroom, can't you? I showed my wife this picture and she almost fainted. We are very frightened, Mr. Grinde. My entire family is afraid. And my son ... my son is being kept alive by machines just because of this piece of shit." He pointed to the first photograph again. "Look here," he continued, pushing the third and final photo in the direction of the detective. "This picture was taken at the same time. Only a few seconds later." It was another photo, the same as the last, taken of his daughter's room. There was one obvious difference though. "See, the ball of light from this photo has moved. It can still be seen here in front of the closet, and larger." Donald conducted the officer's eyes as he pointed from one photo to another.

Detective Grinde was caught off guard and stayed silent. His eyes were trained on the three photographs, studying each of them, one at a time. He sipped from his coffee again and finally looked up at Donald Sterling to speak.

"All right, Mr. Sterling. I'm going to need you to slow down for a minute. Take a breath and tell me what this is all about. I'm very sorry, but I'm having a really hard time understanding what this has to do with a crime."

Donald took a deep breath and stood up from his chair. He glanced at the clock on the wall, which read

1:30 p.m. He paced back and forth across the entire width of the detective's office, wearing away at the oval rug that covered the marble flooring.

"Mr. Sterling," the detective interjected, standing up from his chair and chipping out his cigar in the ashtray, "can I interest you in a glass of water? You don't look too well." Donald shook his head, too anxious to even consider such a thing. "Now look here," the detective said, "I certainly don't want to be wasting your precious time. I would hope that you don't have plans to waste mine either."

"No, no, I don't want to waste your time, detective. That isn't why I'm here." Donald adjusted his glasses and took a seat once again. "Please let me explain better." Detective Grinde slowly returned to his chair, clasped his hands, and placed them on the desk in front of him.

"My wife and I moved to Clover Springs in 1977. We relocated from right here in the city. We have three children, Mr. Grinde. Three!" He became animated. "People warned me about the house. One man warned me and he was already dead, apparently." The detective looked puzzled. "My children … they started seeing things in the big oak tree outside. Our family dog is very intimidated by the house and we found her in the attic."

Donald hesitated as the two men silently rated each

other's sanity. "No one was at home!" he explained, as if it should be obvious. "No one put the dog into the God damn attic. Don't you see? The dog was in the attic and she was a nearly full grown golden retriever." Donald intensified his gaze at the man sitting across the desk. "My son, detective. My son is only 16 years old. He was only 15 when this son of a bitch took him away from us." He pointed at the first photograph again and the smell of foul body odour began to fill the room. "My son told us that he didn't like the house at all. He said that there was something not right there. And we didn't listen to him. We ignored his cry for help and then he got sick. He wanted to leave the house, but he got really sick, and then …" Donald paused and became a tad emotional. The detective stayed silent and listened intently. "And then he got hurt." A tear rolled down his cheek. "I truly believe that the image in this photograph is responsible for hurting my young son, detective. Now he's in a coma. We can't hardly afford to keep him alive. Someone has to pay for this detective. I need you to make someone pay." Donald broke down in front of the officer and shook as he sobbed.

Detective Grinde tried to display sympathy. "Let me get this straight, Mr. Sterling. You're telling me that the images in these photos have somehow hurt your son? That your dog is going up to the attic by herself, and that balls of light are moving around your daughter's bedroom; is that right?" Donald buried his head into his hands and couldn't even respond. The detective attempted to achieve a better understanding of the disgruntled man's testimony. "Now you understand, of course, Mr. Sterling, that these photo's don't provide much proof of your bold allegations. How do I know that these pictures haven't been tampered with? How exactly am I supposed to know if they have been manipulated in any way? I mean, these light anomalies I see in these two photos here, they could simply be exposure or development issues."

Donald interjected. "But I am a professional and successful photographer, detective. I would know if I developed the film incorrectly, now wouldn't I?"

"Well yes, I suppose you would, Mr. Sterling. But this photo of the image on your outside bench. This could be your wife for all I know. Or a friend visiting and sitting there enjoying a cup of coffee."

"In the blowing snow? In the freezing temperatures?" Donald attempted to reason with the official.

"Mr. Sterling," Detective Grinde strove for an ending to the meeting, "this evidence does not indicate a crime. And even if it did, I would need more proof." He hesitated, and then continued. "That is, if what you are telling me is true, Mr. Sterling. You're claiming that these three images represent abnormalities that are outside of this world. That your house is haunted and that these are ghosts of some sort, is that right?" Donald remained distraught. "I'm very sorry, Mr. Sterling, but this is not a police matter. I don't think that I can help you in any way. I hope that you and your family will encounter some better luck soon. You should be with your son, Mr. Sterling … by the sounds of it anyway."

Donald slowly raised his head, took off his glasses, and wiped the tears from his face. He leaned over and collected the three photographs from Detective Grinde's desk and returned them to his leather portfolio folder.

"Well then, I can see now that I have indeed wasted your time, detective. I apologize for the inconvenience. I'll be leaving now, thank you." Donald looked away, collected his belongings, and turned to exit the detective's office.

"Now wait," the officer stopped him. "I told you that *I* couldn't help you, Mr. Sterling, but I know someone who might just be able to." The investigator reached into the left-hand drawer of his office desk and pulled out a business card, which he handed to Donald. "Give this lady a call. She is a friend of mine. She specializes in activity similar to the claims that you are reporting. Mention my name. She will help you. I'm sure of it."

Donald reached out and took the card from the

detective's hand. He placed it into his jacket pocket and didn't read it.

"Thank you, I appreciate your help." Donald turned and left the detective's office. He was shaken to the bone and ragged from exhaustion. He returned to his van and started his long journey home to Clover Springs and his awaiting family. As he merged onto the highway, his head pounded with a migraine headache and new anger flowed throughout his veins.

By the time Donald Sterling had returned home, it was nearing 4:15 in the afternoon. He seemed to have undergone a change in attitude and demeanour during his journey. Subconsciously, he looked over to the porch on his way up the driveway, and after parking, gazed at the big oak in the backyard. He entered through the side entrance and removed his sopping wet shoes, leaving his jacket on as it dripped rain water onto the floor. Barbara and the girls came running to him with their arms flailing, as they were overjoyed and eager to give him a massive hug.

"Yay! Daddy, you're finally back home!" Amanda's face glowed with happiness.

"Did you bring us anything, Dad?" Mary added, as she wrapped her arms around her father.

Donald set his hands on the girl's shoulders and remained stone faced, as he had been the whole drive home. Barbara stood back and watched her husband as he maintained a look that she rarely saw: loneliness and removal, but also strength and resolution.

"Girls, now that Daddy's home, he's going to need some rest. Why don't you go play in your rooms upstairs and I'll call you when supper is ready?"

The girls smiled and chased each other through the living room and up the stairs. Barbara took a step toward Donald, who still stood frozen in the entranceway. She reached out and grabbed both of his hands in hers. They were cold and clammy and seemed dead in her grasp.

"Well, what did you find out?" she asked in anticipation. "Were they able to help you?" Donald stared right through his wife. "For God's sake, Donald, answer me! What's the matter with you? Did the authorities in the city help you or not? You were gone for so long and we all missed you so. Why are you being like this?"

Donald jerked his right hand away from Barbara's tight grasp, and pushed his eyeglasses tight to his forehead.

"Uh yes," he finally responded. "Yes, they helped me. They told me that I was a nut. That's what they said." He snapped out of his nearly frozen state and walked toward the living room, sitting down on the loveseat. "They gave me a card." He reached into his jacket pocket, removed the card, and tossed it on the end table. "I guess our story is a little hard to believe. I would imagine that the person on that card is a shrink. That's what I think. I wouldn't trust them anyway."

"Donald, you haven't even asked about Richard today. Something's wrong with you. I'm terribly worried about you, honey." Barbara tried to give her husband a hug as he sat, but Donald pushed her away. "Do you see how you're acting? You should be ashamed of yourself."

"You don't think I thought about Rich today!" He raised his voice in anger. "That's all I've bloody well done today Barbara! Jesus Christ!"

Barbara tried to calm her husband. "Okay, okay, I'm sorry. I didn't mean it like that. All I meant is that we need to talk about things. I'm really scared, Donald. I'm scared for the kids. I'm scared for you, honey. And I'm scared for me too. I'm just saying that we need to talk about things … that's all."

Donald stared into blank space for a moment and slowly turned his head up to meet his wife's stare.

"Well, what do you want to talk about?" he said coldly.

"Everything that has happened. Richard's bad accident. Everything! Jesus Donald, Dee-Dee was playing outside this morning with the dog, after you left for the city, and came running in crying because she saw the man in the tree again. We're all so very frightened with this house. The bad things are still happening.

I'm worried about the safety of our family, Donald." Barbara wept and finally finished her rant. "What's left of our family that is."

Donald frowned and refused sympathy toward his wife. Something had changed. He appeared to be a completely different person altogether.

Barbara gambled and pushed more bad news onto her internally furious husband.

"Donald, we received another call from the collection agency. On a Sunday too; can you believe it? They're threatening to take the house away if we don't catch up on our bills. The hospital called also, but not to update us on Rich's condition. No … it was to conveniently explain to us that if we couldn't settle up on our medical commitments that they would be forced to obtain a legal court injunction, which would finally discontinue Richard's medical treatment. They told me that they would be forced to pull the plug on our son, Donald!" Barbara screamed out her last statement. "All that I'm saying is that this house has caused us nothing but grief and sorrow since the day we moved in! It's cold and uncomfortable. The kids are scared and one is fighting for his life." She paused and placed a hand on the side of her husband's neck. "Listen, I know that I have mentioned this to you before, and I know that you weren't too happy when I did, but please Donald … please consider selling this house and we can all move on. We don't owe anything to this town. They owe nothing to us. Please hon, let's get out of here before something else happens. I don't think that I could take it." Barbara shed some more tears and sniffled as she awaited his response. She was afraid of what he would say, but calmly braced herself and stared at him unswervingly.

Donald turned to his wife, who had taken a seat beside him on the love-seat. He shuffled his body along the seat away from her. Barbara watched as his face turned beet red and the veins in his forehead began to constrict.

"Have you gone fucking mad, woman? You want us to move out of here … now?" he yelled into his wife's terrified face, causing her to cower from him. The anger flowed through Donald and he became relentless with his actions.

Barbara had never, in the eighteen years they had been together, experienced this kind of rage from her husband. He was infuriated and seemed possessed. He swung his arms around hysterically as he shouted, nearly striking Barbara on several occasions.

He continued his tirade. "Something in this house tried to kill my son! I'll be damned if I'm going to run away like a cowardly fool without getting even with this bastard! Go, if you want! Go! I don't need you. I won't leave! Not until that son of a bitch pays! I just won't leave! Do you understand me?" Donald paused and was breathing heavily, looking at his wife with apparent hatred. "Are you fucking deaf?" he screamed again. "Do you understand me?"

Barbara nodded quickly as she looked down at the floor. Her blue dress, which she had proudly adorned for her husband's return, wilted and became dull and mute in her mind. Donald huffed one final time and ejected himself from the love-seat. He looked down at his wife for a moment, shook his head, then briskly turned and headed upstairs. Barbara buried her grief-stricken face in her hands once again, and surrendered to her anguish.

Little Amanda Sterling stood, shaken, at the bottom of the stairs and scrutinized her father as he bolted past, ignoring her altogether. Donald continued up the stairs and into the master bedroom, where he slammed the door. All was quiet once more. Barbara lifted her head and turned toward the staircase to see her youngest daughter staring at her. Mary had reacted to the yelling and screaming as well and stood at the top of the stairs. She had been in her room, listening to music on her radio, but could still hear the commotion. Barbara's make-up had run down her face and streaked her usual outer beauty. Her mouth hung open as she contemplated what she was going to say to Amanda.

"Mommy?" Amanda said, eager to share some positive news. "I was supposed to give you a message." Barbara focused intently on her daughter's words. "Dortie just told me that you and Daddy are going to get a visitor. She said that it could be soon and that you should be ready. Dortie told me that you and Daddy would like this visitor, but she made sure I told you to be ready."

10
Anomalous Windfall

June 5, 1979

It seemed an eternity with little incident. The visitor Amanda had warned them about hadn't come. Lately Donald had retreated to the confines of the basement. He wasn't taking on many jobs recently, but seemed to always have work to do. The husband and father of three had not lashed out at his wife, nor children for that matter, since his blow up in mid-March. But he was empty. Donald rarely joined the family for meals anymore. Barbara was growing weary of making up excuses for her husband and explaining away his change in behaviour. Mary in particular was having a hard time with it. She was getting to that age where she was understanding the turmoil that surrounded her daily. Both girls excelled in school though, and had graduated to their next grade the month before. Neither of the girls would ever dare speak about the strange occurrences within their house while at school. Mary was well aware that she would, most likely, be judged and ridiculed, but it was Amanda's extreme naivety that resulted in an unassertive, common-place attitude and ignorant silence.

Financial issues were still dire and Barbara knew that the end was near. Three more months … maybe, and then they would lose the house and their son and have next to nothing left. Richard had been in a coma for more than a year and a half. He was slowly losing his body weight and had appeared sickly during Barbara's recent visits. Depression shrouded the mother of three, who now couldn't manage to get through to her husband and was quickly losing control of her imagined life and the successful upbringing of her children.

The two girls prepared themselves for bed as Barbara Sterling cleaned up the kitchen after yet another supper Donald did not attend. She listened as the basement door opened and closed and feared that her husband was coming to the kitchen angry. After a short period of time, she realized that he had, more than likely, walked through the living room and gone upstairs. Barbara turned off the lights and headed up herself, visiting the girl's rooms and kissing them both goodnight. She stood outside her own room and noticed the bedside light had already been switched off, as there was only complete darkness to be seen underneath the door. She retreated downstairs to her office to write for a bit.

By 10:45 p.m., Barbara had lost track of time. Her creative nectars were flowing through her and she had written over thirty-five pages. She shut off her desktop light and left the room, closing the door behind her. As she turned left to head to the stairs, she stopped and tilted her head slightly. Tugging on the sleeve of her long cotton blouse, and scratching her arm, she listened intently. She could hear a noise coming from somewhere within the house. It was muted, but evident. Barbara changed direction and moved toward the closed basement door. She put her left ear to the door and could hear a distinct banging sound resonating from below. Barbara's curiosity got the best of her and she needed to investigate. Perhaps Donald had decided to work some more. She slowly opened the basement door. It creaked. Barbara began to perspire as she realized that the basement was dark and leaned over to flick on the light.

The noise became louder now that the door was

open. It sounded like a damaging clang within an enclosed space. Barbara's heart started to race as she descended the stairs. Once at the bottom, she scanned the spacious empty area quickly and turned toward the corner of the room, where she had found Richard. Seeing nothing that was out of the ordinary, Barbara turned her attention toward the laundry room, from which the noise was definitely echoing. She entered the door-less room and flicked on the light, holding her breath as she did so. Barbara could see now. The noise was coming from the clothes dryer. The knocking inside was intense and the frightened woman slowly moved her hand toward the handle. She pulled the door open and the light inside illuminated the contents, which rattled to a stop within the drum. Barbara slowly leaned over and looked inside. She shuddered at her surprise discovery. It was a football. A deflated football. The exact same deflated football that Richard had chewed on, breaking his own jaw. The stains of dark blood were still apparent. This was the very same deflated football that her husband had thrown away the very same night of Richard's unfortunate episode. That was nearly two years ago, she thought to herself. Terrified, Barbara removed the football from the dryer, stood up, turned the dial to off, and closed the door. She looked down at the ball and tears forced their way out of her eyes. She wondered why her husband would do this. Why would be play such a cruel prank? Even in his condition, this would certainly cross the line. She walked up the stairs and closed the door after shutting off the light. Still holding the football, she became conflicted about even approaching her angry husband with her findings. Then she realized ... maybe this wasn't his doing at all. It was conceivable that this was yet another cautionary signal from the mysterious visitors, who continued to claim the Sterlings' house as their very own. Either way, someone or something was playing a sick joke.

After depositing the football in the outside trash can, Barbara made her way up the stairs and into the master bedroom where Donald was sleeping. She quietly disrobed and climbed under the blankets, ensuring that she didn't interrupt her husband. She looked over to the wall clock, which was illuminated by the moon's light piercing through the window. It read eleven o'clock. Barbara lay on her back and stared at the ceiling, trying to understand her latest experience. After twenty-two agonizing minutes, her mind retired and she fell asleep.

The air in the Sterlings' house thickened and cooled off quickly. Even the usual clamours were non-existent on this particular night. Barbara and Donald slept peacefully on their king-sized red mahogany bed. Their bodies had moved closer together as a result of their dreams. Much closer than when Barbara had joined her husband earlier. They faced each other, about eighteen inches apart, and shared each other's breath.

At precisely 4:26 a.m., a glowing brightness illuminated the Sterlings' master bedroom. It hovered over the bed as a large orb and glued itself to the white stuccoed ceiling. The brightness throughout the room caused Barbara's eyes to squint tightly, even when still closed. She woke, still on her left side, and stared at her husband only inches away. He also stirred. His eyes met Barbara's and they looked at each other in fear. Unable to speak, they turned their bodies to view the glowing light above the bed. The radiant sphere was the size of a basketball. Its core pulsated, sending white beams of light in all directions. As it throbbed to the discrete rhythm of a heartbeat, it seemed to contain a faded and muffled sound. Once they had turned to their backs, Barbara and Donald realized that they were unable to move their bodies any longer. They turned their heads, looking sideways at each other, clearly terrified. Donald also showed her a deep compassion that hadn't been evident for weeks.

Barbara tried hard to speak, but it proved to be challenging.

"W-what is happening to us?" she managed to mutter her question in Donald's direction.

Donald also struggled with his words and tried to respond to his wife, but could not, managing only to glance in Barbara's direction.

Barbara questioned, in her mind, if she was really awake. It seemed like another nightmare, or even worse, another dose of their present reality. This experience was surreal. This couldn't be happening, she thought. It was far too abnormal to exist as genuine. Nothing, though, could have prepared them for what they saw next.

The light began to increase in size but dim slightly, allowing the Sterlings to view it even easier. At that moment, the orb of light (now the size and appearance of a young human being) manifested as a child. The two parents looked at the anomaly in complete fascination. It was a boy, around ten years old. Barbara tried not to cry as she recognized the adolescent boy who was plastered against her bedroom ceiling. Donald recognized him too, even without the aid of his glasses, which sat on the bedside table along with his anxiety medication. It was their young son, Richard. He appeared with a smile on his face, looking much younger than his present state. He was quite pleased and comfortable, wide-eyed and looking superficially intelligent. The Sterlings stared helplessly up at their son as he looked down on them. The sound that resonated from the bright apparition grew very shallow and throbbed to a steady beat. There was little to no movement and a good thirty seconds passed in what felt like an hour. The boy began to shift his glowing eyes left and right, scanning his bewildered and frightened parents one at a time. A high childish voice escaped the apparition they recognized as Richard Sterling. The boy's small lips didn't move as the sound forced its way down from the ceiling of their bedroom.

"*It's okay, Mommy,*" the voice said in a monotone manner. "*Everything is going to be all right. Don't be scared, Daddy, because everything is just fine.*"

The Sterlings listened and stared up at the awesome and immense brightness. Barbara's skin crawled as she watched in disbelief. Donald's usually squinted eyes were twice their normal size. He tried once again to talk, but was only able to open his mouth halfway and move his tongue slightly.

The voice resonated, once more. "*Dig the tree, Daddy. Dig the tree and everything will be all right. Go outside and just dig the tree and everything will be fine.*"

The light that emanated from the young boy intensified. The Sterlings felt as if their bodies were being forced down into their bed. They watched, powerlessly, as the vision of their young son began to disappear into the ceiling. Barbara managed one lone tear, which rolled down her cheek. With a discreet crackle and one last intense flash, the entity was gone. Barbara felt some release from her confinement and looked over to Donald through the darkness. His eyes were closed and his breath was now shallow. She couldn't begin to fathom what had just happened in their bedroom. How could Donald be asleep again? She questioned her own sanity, looking back up to the ceiling and wondering if she had just woken from a dream.

"Donald! Wake up!" She forcefully shook her husband, dismissing her current worries about him. "Donald, what just happened? Donald, please." She continued to shake him back and forth. "What was that? It looked like Rich … it was Rich, wasn't it? Oh my God, please Donald."

Donald finally woke up and responded. He looked over to his wife, surprised and shocked by the sudden interruption to his sleep. Within a few short seconds, an unimpressed glare shrouded his face and he stared angrily at his disorderly wife. Leaning over and grabbing his glasses, he put them on and glanced over Barbara's shoulder toward the alarm clock on her nightstand. It read 4:50 in the morning. He sighed deeply.

"Well, I guess I'm up now." He looked deep into Barbara's eyes through the limited natural light from the window. "I might as well get up now. Right?" he asked sharply, throwing the covers off, spinning out of the bed, and grabbing his robe, which was draped over the chair near the window. Barbara stared at her husband in fright. It was as if he didn't, or couldn't, recall the traumatic experience that had just occurred. She cowered under her covers and listened as her husband grumbled to himself. He grabbed his glasses and put them on.

Donald looked out of the large window toward the back corner of the yard and peered at a light anomaly standing by the big oak tree. The light from the full moon was illuminating the tree just right. He reached up and rubbed his eyes, keeping his penetrating gaze on the vision outside. Donald looked back over to Barbara, whose body shook in despair, sobbing and clutching her covers to her neck. He glanced through the window again, tying the belt on his robe, and turned to exit the bedroom. Misty entered when the door opened, jumping onto the bed to console her mistress. Misty licked Barbara's face as the tears flowed from her eyes. She looked down lovingly at her pet through her anguish and stroked Misty's fur.

Donald walked down to the kitchen and opened up the refrigerator, reaching for the milk. He swigged it directly from the bottle and wiped his wet lips with his sleeve before returning it to its chilled storage. Walking to the side landing, he slipped on his shoes and exited the house, heading out into the dark early morning. Sunrise was still an hour and a half away at this time of year, but Donald continued around the side of the house and out into the backyard. He looked toward the oak tree. The lighted figure was still there, motionless. Without any hesitation, Donald marched toward the tree with a determination, never releasing his gaze from the brightness at the end of the yard. Once he came within fifteen feet, he stopped and was able to see clearer definition of the apparently spiritual being. It was a large man, with a blank expression, who hovered twelve inches or so above the ground. An illuminated energy was being emitted from his insides, out through the surface of his tall, broad body, slicing through the cool early morning air. He wore old tattered clothing, devoid of any colour. The man stood four feet away, to the left of the big oak tree and on the opposite side of the tire swing. There was a long metal spade beside him, spiked into the ground. It stuck out of the earth with its handle pointing to the sky on a thirty-five degree angle. The man slowly turned his head toward the shovel and pointed directly at it. Donald stared in amazement at the manifestation. He thought back to the research he had done in the library and imagined that this man had to be the ghost of Charles Murphy. After just a few more amazing seconds, the image faded away and completely disappeared into thin air, right in front of a hypnotized Donald. He stood, frozen to the ground in the chilly morning darkness.

Donald fought with himself. He tried hard to exist as he was, but something prevented him from it, and worse, he was unable to explain his feelings of remorse to others—to his frustrated and loving family in particular. He felt as if he were trapped, confined and sinking much deeper into the black hole that existed within his soul. Shivering in fear, Donald advanced on the long shovel, which remained sticking out of the ground. He grabbed ahold of it and used some force to remove its blade from the solid ground beneath the massive tree. Standing with the spade, which he gripped with both hands, Donald focused on the spot in the ground where the tool had penetrated. He felt greatly compelled to dig in the spot and reared up tall before driving the shovel deep into the weathered ground. Relentless with his actions, the man dug feverishly into the earth beneath him, tossing the soil off to one side. He began to dig faster and faster, ignoring the jarring pain that shot through his shoulders as he hit tree roots with every inch he uncovered. He was determined though and the pain wasn't relevant.

Barbara laid in bed, clutching her pillow with her fragile hands and wrapping her left leg over top of her sympathetic dog. An uneventful hour had now passed and she couldn't muster the motivation to force her exhausted body out of her bed. She looked over to the clock on the wall, which now read 5:56. The girls wouldn't be awake for another hour, but Barbara finally found the courage to get up and leave the comfort of her warm blankets. She stood and walked to the window, where she could see that the sun was beginning to illuminate the horizon. Her husband was there, in plain sight, under the far oak tree. He was zealously removing the earth from beneath the tree, and she could see that a large hole was developing. Barbara was flabbergasted and couldn't begin to imagine why he would be motivated, at six in the morning, to dig a hole in their backyard. Then it hit her. She remembered that the apparition of her beloved son had mentioned something about "*digging the tree.*" Donald must have surely heard him. He must have actually experienced the exact same psychological ordeal that she had, just over an hour before. They had looked at each other and tried to communicate. He saw it, just like her, she thought, but why had he reacted like he did when he got out of bed? It made no sense. She could see that Donald was still in his dark robe, and watched as he continued hitting roots beneath the tree as he shovelled, sending stinging vibrations up his forearms and throughout his entire body. But he continued, without hesitation or recognition. Barbara quickly pulled her pure white nightgown off over her head, revealing her slender, curvy body. Keeping her eyes on her husband, she pulled on a pair of slacks and one of Donald's over-sized t-shirts. She looked out at Donald one last time. He had stopped shovelling. A gaping hole had appeared in a relatively short period of time and he had fallen to his knees. Barbara quickly ran out of the bedroom and down the stairs, making sure that she wasn't loud enough to wake up the girls. Misty followed closely behind her mistress in anticipation of her breakfast and whimpered as she reached the living room.

Donald, who was on all fours, used his hands to dig at the bottom of the thirty-inch deep hole. It was two feet long and three feet wide. Pulling out handful after handful of mud and dirt, Donald tossed it all aside, hesitating only briefly as Barbara came running toward him. He never looked up at her. Instead, he concentrated on the bottom of the hole. He reached down and tugged at the sides and corners of a large metal box, which had been obviously buried quite a long time ago. Keeping his stone-like expression, he grabbed the sides with both of his hands and tried to pull the box out of the hole. Barbara stopped, three feet away from Donald, and stared down at him, terrified. She was speechless and deathly afraid of even distracting her annoyed man. As she opened her dry lips to speak—to finally confront her husband about his peculiar actions—a shrieking voice prevented her from doing so.

"Mom!" A voice shot through the darkness from an upstairs window. Barbara looked toward the voice, across the yard. "Mom!" Mary's voice projected from the master bedroom. "There's someone on the telephone! It wouldn't stop ringing, so I came and answered the one in your room! It's the hospital! Hurry mom, it's the doctor at the hospital! He really sounds like he needs to tell you something important!"

Barbara turned back to Donald, who continued struggling with the large metal box, which was heavy and awkward. Barbara returned her gaze toward the house and started running as fast as she could through the yard's tall grass, her emotions flowing. She knew there was going to be news about Richard, and recent events led her to believe that the update might be devastating. The sprint was less than a hundred feet, from the tree to the side door, but it seemed to take a millennium in Barbara's mind. She broke through the door and ran to the kitchen without removing her shoes, grabbing the telephone hanging on the wall. Mary hung up the upstairs telephone receiver, and she and Amanda came down, running through the living room and waited quietly by the entrance to the kitchen. Taking a couple of quick, deep breaths, Barbara calmed and introduced her presence.

"H-hello?" she said meekly.

"Mrs. Sterling? Hello, this is Doctor Collins from

Mercy General Hospital. I'm sorry to disturb you at this hour, but I had to let you know, as soon as I could, that something has happened with Richard."

"Oh my God!" Barbara shrieked. "What's happened now?" Her words were slurred by emotion. "Oh please don't tell me that we've lost him! Please!"

Dr. Collins answered the frenzied mother. "Wait. Please. Usually, as you know, I would ask that you come down here to discuss the circumstances, but I understand that this news needs to be communicated to you over the telephone. Mrs. Sterling, Richard was being checked on, by the nurse, at about four o'clock this morning. He had finally woken up from his lengthy coma."

The aura around Barbara brightened immediately.

"Mrs. Sterling," the doctor continued, "we responded to your son's condition as quickly as possible, but then he slipped into cardiac arrest and we lost his pulse."

"Nooooo!" Barbara screeched through the telephone. "Nooooo! Why him? Why my Rich?" Her two daughters, standing tensely in the doorway, grabbed each other's arms and took a step back in fear.

"Mrs. Sterling? No, no!" Doctor Collins interrupted her despair. "Richard is still alive, Mrs. Sterling! We were able to revive him. We worked on him for forty-five minutes and he seemed to be gone, but then he came back to us again. He's alive, Mrs. Sterling! We have sedated him and he seems to be resting peacefully for the moment and breathing on his own. It was very strange, Mrs. Sterling ... like he had taken a short break from his living being and then returned at his own convenience. Something told me to keep working on him and not to give up—something that I've never experienced before. It told me to continue trying."

"Oh thank God!" Barbara bounced back and forth with her emotions. "He's alive? He's really alive. Oh yes, thank you, Doctor Collins. Thank you so much. My baby's alive!"

"Come down to the hospital, Mrs. Sterling," the doctor reassured the overjoyed woman. "You and your husband have been looking forward to this moment for a long time now. He won't be awake for at least an hour ... maybe two. It depends. But he's alive Mrs. Sterling. Congratulations!"

Meanwhile, Donald managed to remove the metal box from the hole in the ground and pushed it toward the tree's massive trunk. The box had two hinged releases and wasn't locked. Donald unlatched the box, and folded the top of the old dirty metal crate backward on its hinges. He looked down at a miraculous sight. The box was filled high with old bank notes, rare coins, silver, and many pieces of paper that appeared to be some sort of a banker's bonds. There must have been nearly $10,000 of monetary value in the box when it was buried. Donald began to sift through the newly discovered wealth. The reaction on his face remained neutral, but Donald knew, all too well, that the contents of the box would surely be worth much more now even than when they had been buried.

11
Thickened Adversary

June 21, 1979

Nearly a month had passed since the peculiar events that changed the fortunes of the Sterling family. After Donald had dragged the box of currency to the house, he left it at Barbara's feet and sat down on the chair in the living room. Barbara didn't ask questions then and hadn't since. It was agreed that the currency was to remain the property of the Sterling family, as there was no link to any other owner and the most valuable currency was, after all, found on the Sterlings' property. Once it was all converted, the Sterling family were richer by $33,000, a tremendous amount of money for the times. Barbara used the funds, without any input from Donald, to pay the medical bills for Richard in full, and to clear up the debt owed on their property, including any back taxes. Donald remained secluded, in the basement or up in the master bedroom, away from his family.

Richard was alive but not yet out of the woods. He was able to see and react to the events surrounding him, but he was unable to speak and remained too weak to move his arms and legs much. The doctors were bewildered as to the cause of his muteness but continued monitoring his progress as he rehabilitated. He was able to eat soft foods now, things like oatmeal, soup, ice cream, and pudding, which helped his malnourished body heal from its near two-year hiatus. The Sterling family had visited him daily for the last three weeks. Richard smiled at his sisters and was able to grip his mother's hand. Even Donald had gone to the hospital. He spoke to his son, but in a precise monotone fashion, showing little joy for his son's recovery. Richard would look anguished, but he was still unable to really communicate his emotions.

On this particular Thursday afternoon, it began to rain outside. It started as a shower, but soon the wind gained strength and the heavens poured. The Sterlings had just returned home from visiting Richard in the hospital and Donald retired to the basement, still distant and angry. Barbara would regularly confront her husband in the feeble attempt to work things out. Donald wanted no part of it, snapping at her or simply leaving the room in almost frantic frustration. He rarely spoke up anymore and the children were beginning to notice. The man of the family remained the predominant concern for everyone. His disengagement endangered the well-being of the entire family unit and all involved were beginning to question whether he would ever snap out of his negative funk. His attitude was terrifyingly similar to the temperament Richard had been held hostage by.

Barbara held Amanda's hand and tucked her in for an afternoon nap in her bedroom. After a kiss on the cheek, she headed down, meeting Mary on the stairs. The two embraced and Mary continued upstairs to hang out in her bedroom. Barbara poured herself a glass of water from the tap in the kitchen and headed to her office to write, with Misty at her ankles following her into the room. She closed the door. The tensions and sadness had subsided for the moment. At least mostly. The house had been quiet lately. Richard was recovering, and financially, they were in an unfamiliar (and welcome) lucrative state of affairs. It was evident that the thick energy that existed in the house and around the Sterlings' property was an evil presence—a hurtful and malicious presence that seemed relentless and offered no motive.

Mary sat in her bedroom as the white gloved hands of her Minnie Mouse wall clock pointed to 2:54. The rain outside pelted down on the house relentlessly, drenching the outside landscape. The young girl was nearly 14 already, and old enough to consider the events since Richard's accident. She would keep quiet, most of the time, when it came to the extraordinary occurrences throughout the living space, but make no mistake, Mary was only displaying a courageous, valiant front for her family and the persistent powers that seemed to exist in her house.

Today, she wore a light green, suede jumpsuit with unseen knee-high socks. The radio was turned up slightly to mask the sound of the rain. Mary listened to one of her favourite songs by the Bee Gees: "How Deep Is Your Love?" As she danced around her bedroom, an unusual sound began to resonate through the walls. It interrupted the steady reverberations from the music and even overpowered the pounding rainfall on the rooftop. Mary turned the volume of her transistor down to listen closer. She could hear a noise coming clearly from the bathroom next door to her bedroom. The two rooms shared an interior wall, so Mary shuffled to her closet and slowly opened the doors. Her heart raced in anticipation of what she might discover. She slid her clothes hangers aside to expose the dividing wall. The sound from the other side of the wall broadcast a racket that mimicked the sound of the drum from a marching band. It wasn't a drum sound, though. It was more of a "ticking" sound, and it contained its very own unnerving and distinct beat. Tick-tickity-tick … Tick-tickity-tick … Tick-tickity-tick, the noise continued. The sound was distinct and Mary couldn't help but notice that the hairs stood up on her arms, as an electricity seemed to flow through the closet wall.

Mary backed out of her closet and turned toward her closed bedroom door. Once her door opened, the sound from the bathroom stopped abruptly. Mary continued the short distance down the hall to the bathroom door, which was cracked open. The light was off. Mary's eyes grew big and her palms began to sweat as she pushed the bathroom door open and flicked on the light. The room was empty, but her eyes immediately focused on the marble vanity, which held an unusual sight. Two toothbrushes lay on the counter, side by side and in perfect alignment with each other. They hung over the vanity by two inches. Mary looked down and knew right away what they represented. The ticking sound that she'd heard were these two toothbrushes. They were lined up like drumsticks, and without experimentation, Mary knew that the sound that they made when striking the marble would clearly mimic the noise she'd heard. She looked over to the shower curtain, which was closed, and a lump developed in her throat. She cautiously slid her feet along the floor and placed her hand on the brown plastic curtain, pulling it back with an abrupt jerk. Thankfully the bathtub was unoccupied, and the teenager breathed a sigh of relief. The feeling didn't last. Mary thought of her little sister, Amanda, in her own room and almost immediately started to panic. Perhaps it was Amanda who'd placed the toothbrushes after playing a very precise beat. Maybe Mary's mother and father had come up from downstairs to use the washroom and were playing a trick. Mary left the toothbrushes where they were, shut off the lights, and turned down the hall toward Amanda's room to confront and question her.

Mary only made it two steps out of the bathroom when she stopped in her tracks, frozen to the flowery carpet runner on the hardwood floor. Blocking her path was a perfect sphere of light. It was about the size of a medicine ball and three feet off of the floor. Mary held her breath and the hairs on her neck reached out in all directions. She wasn't exuding any great fear, but the electricity in the hallway was definitely evident—an immense and powerful energy that affected all of Mary's senses. She could see the ball of light easily and feel the static on her body. Her nose picked up a distinct burning sensation. It was the smell of scorching hairs. Her ears picked up a low humming noise that resonated from the ball in front of her, and even Mary's sense of taste was greatly affected. Each time she swallowed, she could taste an acidic impression that she would compare, in her mind, to eating rust. She backed up and slowly retreated into the bathroom, keeping her eyes on the hovering orb. She turned the light back on and closed the door tightly. Breathing heavy, Mary spun around and looked at the vanity. The toothbrushes were gone. They were now sitting vertically in their holder on the end of the counter. Her eyes then caught something strange above the vanity. The large, five-foot mirror on the wall had fogged up, as if someone had taken a hot shower, and there was writing in it. The writing had clearly been scribbled with a small crooked finger. Mary recited the phrase on the mirror to herself.

"I saw a man who wasn't there." Mary became tremendously frightened. She knew those words. She heard her mother speak of them and how they'd appeared on her typewriter paper. She knew that those precise words had also appeared, verbatim, on her sister's bedroom wall, written in lipstick. Mary began to feel agitated. She took her hands and feverishly rubbed the mirror to erase the words. In great desperation, she knew that there was more danger and again bolted from the washroom to find her parents and warn them.

The light was still there. It hadn't moved, only increased in size. It now looked more like a glowing, two-foot-by-three-foot picture window. The brightness covered the pathway down the hallway and seemed to block Mary's escape path. Extremely alarmed now, Mary held her breath, squinted her eyes, and dashed forward toward the glare, through it, and out the other side. As Mary's body penetrated the energy, it jolted sideways, in an instant, into the side wall where it disappeared. Mary didn't look back. She ignored her sister's closed bedroom door and grabbed the banister, hurrying down the stairs.

"Mom!!" she screamed loudly. "Come quick! There's something upst—"

As Mary's foot touched down on the fifth step, her hand was ripped away from the safety of the banister and her body was propelled left, where it smashed hard into the wall, penetrated the wood panelling and breaking through, exposing the studs of the house. Mary's body bounced off the wall and she let out a breathless shout. She landed hard on the seventh step and finally came to rest on the ninth, about halfway down. After a brief moment of shock, Mary was able to let out a horrific scream, which had the entire family running, once more, to the aid of one of their own.

Donald, hearing the commotion upstairs, ran up and pushed open the basement door. His path was intercepted by Barbara, who brushed up against him as she bolted past him toward her crying child. Misty howled and also ran past Donald, ensuring that she didn't come too close to him. Little Amanda Sterling dashed out of her bedroom, after hearing the explosive impact of her sister hitting the wall below her room, and sat on the stair above Mary, consoling her pains and crying along with her. Barbara arrived and pulled the hair out of Mary's eyes.

"Mary, sweetheart, are you okay? Oh my God, what's happened? No, oh God no ... this is not happening again!" Barbara propped Mary's body against her own. "Are you all right dear? Oh, please be all right. How did this happen? Oh my God, Mary, please be all right."

She quickly scanned the area and saw the hole in the wood panelling a few stairs up. Barbara turned and looked back to her husband, who stood in front of the chesterfield and the large picture window facing the front porch. He had a blank expression on his face that lacked any empathy for his daughter's awful misfortune. Barbara looked back to her injured daughter, who was crying hysterically, and began checking Mary's extremities for blood or broken bones.

"I'm okay," cried Mary, "I don't think I hurt myself

really bad, but I'm *so* freaked out." She wrapped her arms around her mother. "I'm so scared, Mom. I don't want to be here anymore. Please! I'm really, really scared, Mom. Richard was right, Mom. He was right all along."

Barbara was finally convinced that Mary was not in an overly dire medical situation, needing a rushed trip to the hospital, but turned back to her husband, who remained standing motionless and unhelpful.

"For God's sake, Donald, call a doctor! Mary is hurting, can't you see? Wake up, dammit! How can you just stand there at a time like this? Go and call a doctor, Donald. Do something, for God's sake."

Donald turned and walked to the telephone in the kitchen, seemingly surrendering to his wife's panicked direction.

"What happened, honey?" Barbara slowly helped Mary to her feet and down the stairs into the living room. She supported most her daughter's weight as they descended, as Mary couldn't put weight on her left leg. "Does your leg really hurt you, honey? Tell me what else is causing you some pain." Barbara maneuvered Mary to the love-seat, where she assisted in lying her down.

Donald hung up the telephone and strolled to the entrance of the living area, where he stopped and fell back into his meaningless stare. Amanda had followed down the stairs and sat on a big chair in the living room, stroking Misty, who had finally calmed down. The pouring rain outside continued and flowed off of the patio overhang like a waterfall. Barbara focused on her middle child with great distress and awaited the arrival of the family doctor, who made house calls around town on a regular basis. She looked back to her husband with a very serious, steadfast look on her face. Her entire disposition frowned in disgust and she confronted Donald, once and for all.

"This ends now!" she commanded. Her voice rose and she screamed at Donald, who had emotionally checked out. "Do you hear me!? This ends now! I'm not putting up with this anymore, Donald!" Amanda remained on full alert, and her heartbeat raced as a result of her mother's tone. Mary continued to weep and tend to the sore points on her body. "If you're not going to help," Barbara continued, "I'll take care of this myself. I don't even need you. Our children are getting hurt, Donald! What in the bloody hell is the matter with you!?"

Donald stared at his wife for a brief moment, then turned and went back down into the basement. The distraught mother started to cry and her attention shifted back to the needs of her two daughters.

Doctor Snyder arrived only fifteen short minutes after Donald made the call. Amanda opened the front door and he entered, dripping wet from the inclement weather outside. Removing his galoshes, coat and hat, he hobbled into the living room to tend to Mary.

"What's happened?" he asked.

"Doctor Snyder, thank you for coming. Mary has had an accident, only twenty minutes ago, on the stairs." She pointed up the staircase and directed Doctor Snyder's eyes to the damage to the wall.

"Lie still now, Mary," the doctor ordered. "Let me take a good look at you. Tell me what is causing you pain, okay?"

"My leg hurts." Mary still wept. "I think everything else is okay, but my leg really hurts."

Doctor Snyder grabbed at Mary's ankle and she let out a howl of pain. After closer inspection of the girl's leg, he provided a speedy diagnosis, which offered some comfort.

"Mary, your ankle only appears to be sprained. Nothing more." The doctor went to his bag where he removed a tensor bandage and wrapped Mary's tender ankle. After he finished, he patted the teenage girl on the head and stood up, facing Barbara. He motioned for her to follow him to a more private place where they could talk, out of earshot of the girls. The two adults walked to the kitchen and stood by the counter. Barbara used her section of it to hold herself up.

"Barbara, where is your husband?" the doctor asked.

"He's downstairs, working in the basement," Barbara said. "Why? Do you need to speak with him as well?"

"No, that won't be necessary." Doctor Snyder paused, looking at his feet for a moment before raising his head and addressing the still horrified mother. "Barbara, I think Mary is going to be just fine. But I really need to ask," his words became uncomfortable, "how would you say that Mary's accident on the stairs occurred?"

"Well, I don't exactly know yet, doctor. Mary hasn't filled me in with the details yet. I just heard a loud crash and came running. She was so scared and hysterical … and why would it matter?" she asked curiously.

After a brief period of communication through eye contact alone, Doctor Snyder answered Barbara.

"Uh … Barbara, when Donald called me on the telephone, he said something that concerned me. I don't know exactly how I should tell you. You may not want to hear it."

"What is it, doctor? What did he say when he called you?" The hairs on Barbara's arms reached for the ceiling once more. "Let me guess, he was an ass to you, wasn't he? He probably told you that I did this, didn't he? That wouldn't surprise me."

The doctor paced briefly to the other end of the kitchen, before turning and moving back toward her, facing her directly and placing his hand on her shoulder.

"Barbara … Donald told me that the 'bitch' had survived the fall and I needed to come right away, because you were getting suspicious. I asked him what he meant, but he hung up on me. Is everything all right with you and Donald? Is there anything that I can do to help?"

"I don't think there is anything that you can do to help, doctor, but thank you anyway."

Barbara stood frozen like a statue and stared blankly into the doctor's chest. Everything was definitely not fine in the Sterlings' everyday lives. All of their emotions seemed to roll like waves on an ocean and their future remained quite uncertain.

12
The Unexpected Visitor

September 12, 1979

Mary's ankle had nearly fully healed. She showed few ill effects from her accident and by now had told her frightened mother the story of what happened that night. She explained the toothbrushes in the washroom upstairs and the ball of light in the hallway. Amanda insisted that it was Dortie's energy that blocked Mary's path. Ignoring her sister, Mary had clarified that she had seen writing on the bathroom mirror and (most importantly) been forcefully pushed down the stairs by something she couldn't see.

It was a Wednesday. Mary and Amanda were

back in school and beginning grades nine and three respectfully. Both girls continued to keep quiet with their peers at school, under their mother's clear advisement. Donald declined an invitation from Barbara to go and visit their Richard, who remained in the hospital and was still unable to communicate. He had grown resilient though. The 17-year-old boy had matured somehow while in his coma. He exuded increased understanding through his eye movements and facial expressions. Barbara decided to drive herself to the hospital, leaving her increasingly distant husband behind.

She arrive mid-morning, carrying a large handbag and wearing a light jacket over top of her white blouse and a pair of long cotton pants that flared out at the bottom of the legs. She proceeded through the double doors of the hospital's main entrance. Barbara had become a fixture throughout the hospital—a genuine regular known by most of the staff, and many of the long-term patients, by name. No one was aware of the desperate situation at home though. She kept two secrets: her estrangement from her husband and the unwanted company that resided in the house with the Sterling family. Barbara was stopped on her way to Richard's room by Walter, the hospital's custodian, a mentally challenged man, in his fifties, who had been employed at the hospital for the past thirty years.

"Hello, Barbara Sterling," Walter greeted the familiar visitor. "How are you today, Barbara Sterling? Are you here to see Richard, I hope? You're not hurt are you, Barbara Sterling?" Walter leaned his mop handle against the wall and reached out to assist his friend. "I can see that there is no Donald Sterling today, right? Donald Sterling did not come today, right Barbra Sterling?"

"No, Walter," Barbara smiled, and placed her hand on the man's shoulder. "I'm not hurt. Mr. Sterling is at home resting today. Yes, I'm here to see my Richard. How is he today? Have you seen him yet?"

"Yes Barbara Sterling, I did see Richard today … just a few minutes ago I think. I saw him, and guess what Barbara Sterling? Guess what?"

Barbara let out an affectionate chuckle, shaking her head at the kind soul.

"What is it Walter? I can't guess. You'll have to tell me."

"Well Barbara Sterling, Richard has something to tell you … yeah, he has something to tell you. You should see."

Barbara looked intensely at the portly cleaning man. "What did you say, Walter?" she asked, insisting on clarity.

"Richard just told me that he had something to tell you. Don't you want to talk to Richard, Barbara

Sterling? He wants to talk to you. He even told me so."

Staring at Walter in shock and udder disbelief, Barbara scanned the reception area and looked back to him. Her adrenaline pulsated throughout her body and she put her hand on Walter's chest, then quickly rushed away.

"Excuse me Walter, it was nice to see you again. Take care of yourself."

Barbara ran past reception and pushed open her son's hospital room door. There was Richard, sitting up in his bed, propped up by two pillows and drinking apple juice from a cup. He looked tired and there were black circles under his eyes.

"H-hi ... Mom." Richard's voice was broken, but his words were angelic to Barbara's ears.

"Hello sweetheart!" The overjoyed mother ran to her son's side. "You can speak again! You can talk, Rich!" Her excitement caused her to bounce as she spoke.

"Y-yes ... Mom, I just sta ... started. Only a ... an hour ago." He was having difficulty enunciating.

Barbara's smile faded and her thoughts reverted to her son's long-term well-being. "Do the doctor's know that you can talk yet, Rich? Have you been able to let the nurses know yet?"

"No Mom, they do ... don't know yet." Richard yawned and appeared to become increasingly sleepy all of a sudden. He reached over to the bedside controls and lowered his bed, bringing his body into a horizontal position. He lay and stared at the ceiling of his hospital room, before closing his eyes and struggling to stay conscious.

"We have to let the doctors know, Rich. I'll go and tell them now. I'll be right back, okay sweetheart?"

"I'm kind of ... t-tired Mom," said Richard. Barbara hesitated before leaving the room and Richard managed to communicate with his mother once again. His words were difficult to understand, but she listened carefully.

"Mom ...did ... did you see me? Did you ... s-see me when I ... visited you and Dad a few ... months ago? I ... was above you and I ... I told you every ... everything was g-going to be okay ... Do you remember?"

Barbara's jaw dropped. She stared silently at her son, who was fading into sleep. She ran out and raised her voice to the reception counter down the hall.

"Hey! Hey, somebody, please come! Rich is talking and he needs help! Please, anyone!"

A nurse ran to the side of Richard Sterling. He had fallen asleep and was thankfully breathing normally. She looked up to Barbara, who had followed and stayed at the room's entrance.

"We sedated him, less than an hour ago. He had just woken up and wrote on his paper that his back was sore. He wasn't speaking then. He ate that banana from his breakfast tray and took a drink of his juice." She pointed to the peel and half-empty cup. "I'm not exactly sure why he reacted so quickly to the medication. He usually only rests during the day and rarely falls asleep this soon after he wakes. He seems fine though Mrs. Sterling. I'll keep my eyes on him and call Doctor Collins to come and examine him when he wakes up." The nurse guided Barbara out of the room. "Why don't you just go home and get some rest? Tell Mr. Sterling the good news that Richard is talking. He is doing much better and I anticipate that he'll be back home with you all soon. Go and tell Mr. Sterling. He'll be so pleased to hear, don't you think?"

Barbara smiled sheepishly, nodded, and hugged the young nurse, once again overcome by her emotions. She thanked the nurse and left the hospital, driving home to greet her next unknown adventure.

Barbara arrived home earlier than usual. She entered the side door, and looking through the kitchen, saw Donald sitting at the dining-room table. He was slurping some soup that he had earlier heated up on the stove. Barbara entered the kitchen and looked at the clock. It was only eleven. She walked into the dining room and hung her purse on the closest chair.

"Rich is talking again, Donald. He even spoke to me." There was no response. Barbara drooped her head, disappointed with her husband's recent lack of love and affection. "This is what we've been waiting for, Donald. Surely you can find some happiness."

Donald looked down at his soup and ladled a spoonful to his wet lips before dropping the spoon into the bowl and addressing his wife.

"That's really great." He spoke softly. "That's great news, Barb. I knew Richard would be all right. I told you that a long time ago, now didn't I?"

Barbara looked wide eyed at Donald, who was remaining sombre and unimpressed. He deliberately tilted his head downward and continued to eat his soup without any hesitation. Although he was always there in his physical state, Donald was withdrawn mentally. It was painfully apparent.

"They say he may come home soon, Donald. Rich is going to need your love and support when he comes home. There's already so much going on around here." Barbara was concerned for her son's welfare, but wasn't sure how to inform her husband of this. "Is Rich going to be okay to come home, Donald?"

Donald pushed his spoon down hard into his bowl, and it clanged as his vegetable soup splashed onto the table. He annunciated each word carefully and delicately. "And what, exactly, is that supposed to mean, Barbara? Do you think I'm going to place a pillow over his face while he sleeps?" His eyes pierced hers.

Barbara stood, stunned by her husband's words. Her heart raced and she struggled with the exact meaning behind his question. The uncanny choice of example in his response made Barbara shake.

"No, of course not." She found the nerve to respond. "I just meant ... with all the activity in the house. Mary just got pushed down the stairs, Donald! She could have been really hurt. You know that there's evil energy here. You admitted it. You said that this house is possessed by the energy of the ... the Murphy family. Why are you shutting us all out? We need you now more than ever, Donald. I can't keep lying to the girls about you. They're not stupid. They see how you're acting, and Richard is going to see it too. Is that what you want?" Barbara's eyes began tearing up once again. "Please Donald, we all need your help. Help yourself, for God's sake."

After a long pause, Donald picked up his bowl, still looking at Barbara, and walked past her to the kitchen where he deposited the still quarter-full bowl of soup into the sink. He turned and glared back at Barbara before walking down the hall, through the living room, and up the stairs, where he locked himself in the master bedroom. Barbara sat at the dining room table and simply wept, feeling defeated and lonely.

After she had cleaned up the kitchen and tidied up the boots and shoes at the side entrance, Barbara retired to her office to write. The two girls would need to be picked up at school in a few hours and she needed to take her mind off of the whirlwind of activities that consumed her current lifestyle. She entered her office and walked to the window, which overlooked the backyard from ground level.

She scowled at the large oak in the back corner of the yard, and then saw a woman standing by the tire swing. She was short and very stout, wearing an extra-large one-piece garment, with a multi-coloured floral print. Barbara could see from the window that the lady had extremely large breasts, which caused her dress to hang like a drape over her body. She wore sandals on her bare feet and stood motionless by the tree. Before Barbara could react to the sight, the woman turned slowly and faced the window, seemingly staring directly into her frightened eyes. Barbara felt strongly that she was witnessing yet another apparition on her personal property, but this time, something was noticeably different. This woman had a completely solid appearance and was more defined than that of her predecessors. The strange woman in the yard began walking toward the house, keeping her eyes on the picture window Barbara was peering out of. Stunned by fear, she watched as the woman, weighing at least three hundred pounds, waddled past her sightline and down the side of the house. Barbara couldn't breathe. She ran to her office door and opened it up, looking through the dining room and toward the kitchen, unsure of what to expect. It was much too quiet. Barbara took a few steps out of the office and walked to the basement door. She glanced over at the closed door and continued forward, turning right and down the hall toward the side entrance. Barbara raised herself on to her tiptoes and glanced out of the window at the top of the side door. She couldn't see anybody, and it appeared as if the woman had completely disappeared. Barbara slowly dropped her heels back to the floor and looked down to the doorknob, as an intense anxiety coursed through her body. She reached out to turn the handle, just as a forceful knocking resonated from the front door. Barbara jumped back and let out a squeal as she looked down the hall toward the source of the racket. She slowly walked toward the front entrance and froze in her tracks as the banging began again, this time much more intensely. Barbara found it difficult to continue, but inched forward, took a deep breath, and opened up the door.

The strange woman Barbara had seen from the office window stood on the front steps. She was massive, obesely shaped, and had large folds of severely freckled skin covering her arms, neck, and face. The woman, who seemed to be in her fifties, smelt like sage and wore bifocals. Barbara stood shocked and remained in her defensive posture. She finally spoke.

"Yes, can I help you?"

Misty, laying by the fireplace, looked up, let out a faint growl, and then returned to sleep. In the eyes of the family pet, the stranger at the door didn't seem to be any immediate danger.

The woman peered directly through Barbara and scanned the Sterlings' living space before entering the house, barely fitting through the door. She slipped off her sandals and brushed past the woman of the house to stand facing the vast living room. She took four deep breaths through her nose and smiled.

"What do you think you're doing here?" Barbara was alarmed by the stranger's blatant insistence at penetrating the house's interior.

"So this is the old Murphy house," she said with astonishment, keeping her back to Barbara. "I never thought I would see the day."

Barbara took a step toward the round woman, who turned around with a massive grin on her face.

"Well this is fascinating, now isn't it, Barbara? I can call you 'Barbara', can't I? Oh lady, you have no idea how long I've waited for this." She continued to scan the residence.

Barbara looked at the woman in shock. "How do you know my name?" she asked. "Who in the hell are you and why are you standing, uninvited, in my home?"

The woman realized she had digressed. "Oh, oh ... my apologies, Barbara." She reached out her huge hand. "My name is Prescott. Maria Prescott."

Barbara cautiously shook her hand and wrinkled her forehead in wonderment.

"I've heard of you before ... but I don't know how, or when I've ever met you. Do we know each other? I feel that I should remember somehow."

Maria laughed with a low-toned, almost vindictive jab in her voice. "Of course we don't know each other, you silly, silly girl. We've just met, now haven't we? I think you would know if you had met me before, now wouldn't you?" The woman seemed to be ridiculing Barbara and belittling her intelligence.

"What can I do for you, Mrs. ... Prescott, is it?"

Maria paused and viewed the bewildered-looking Barbara up and down. Then she turned and walked to the middle of the living room, where she made her intentions known.

"Barbara, I have done a great deal of research on your house and property over the years, and I have to tell you, it's exactly how I expected it to look." She peered back at Barbara, who remained at the entrance. "The inside I mean. I've seen the outside a thousand times, of course."

Terrified by the woman's chilling words, Barbara insisted on some clarification.

"What do you mean? Have you been stalking my house? My family? Who are you?!"

The woman took a few steps back toward Barbara, and leaned in closer to her, softening her voice. "You already know who I am, Barbara, now don't you? I told you, just a minute ago."

Barbara grew frustrated and demanded an answer. "Why are you here, Mrs. Prescott?"

"Barbara, I am a spiritual medium. I've come to help you. To help your family."

"A medium?" repeated Barbara. "You mean, you're like a psychic or something?"

Maria smiled and leaned in closer. "Let me make myself clear, Barbara. All real mediums have some sort of psychic ability, but not all psychics are mediums, do you understand me?" Barbara nodded slightly and the woman continued. "So, because I've already told you that I'm a medium, I believe that you've actually answered your own question ... now haven't you, dear?" After a momentary pause, Maria turned her back to Barbara and proceeded down the hallway. "I thought so," she confidently said, as she disappeared around the far corner and moved into the large kitchen. She shuffled while she walked and her feet scraped like sandpaper along the floor.

Barbara then remembered where she had recognized the woman's name from. It was on the business card Donald had brought home from his visit to the city. Maria Prescott—a unique name and quite difficult to easily forget. Barbara followed the overweight woman into the kitchen and through to the dining room area, where she managed to squeeze herself into a chair, making herself right at home.

"How did you hear about us?" asked Barbara. "Are we the new gossip topic around town or something?"

Maria looked up over the top of her glasses and stared sharply at Barbara Sterling.

"Well now, Barbara, that's an unusual question, don't you think? Your husband, Donald, called me ... just a few days ago." She reached up from her chair, placed her hand on Barbara's thin waist, and looked up at her. Her pupils dilated as she raised her eyes, stretching her face into an oval shape. "I'm so sorry to see that the two of you aren't communicating with one another. That's a shame, now isn't it?"

13
Anticipated Returns

September 12, 1979

Maria Prescott pried herself out of the dining-room chair and walked through the doorway leading to the hall where the main level bathroom and office were. She looked up to the high ceiling and then back down to the floor before addressing Barbara Sterling.

"I need to check your house, Barbara. I need to look it through ... each and every room. I feel a presence here. It's actually a presence that I haven't felt in quite some time. Your house is haunted, Barbara." She graciously paused and let this sink in. "You already know that, now don't you?" Barbara closed her eyes and nodded. The woman continued, "You mustn't follow me, Barbara. I will need you to stay right here. This energy that exists in your home is displaying distinct signs of awareness. Most of the energy is choosing to hide but some is not. I need you to stay here while I tour your home and attempt to have them communicate with me. Do you understand? I won't take up too much of your time." She glanced at a gold pocket watch that hung around her neck from a thin, finely linked chain.

"No, I don't understand," Barbara said, making it clear that she was struggling with the purpose of the outsider's visit. "Why have you come? What is it that you feel you will be able to achieve here?"

Maria shrugged her spacious shoulder blades and promptly answered her.

"You have a problem here; am I right Barbara? Surely you are smarter than that. This house has brought you and your family great despair. I sense many accidents and pain. Lots of anguish and sadness here. Your husband has asked for help and I can help you. That's all. Please let me know if you want me to leave. The spirits that are in your house would be quite satisfied … but it is your house after all. At least that's what you think, isn't it Barbara?"

Barbara had an alarmed look on her face and

looked down the hallway toward the staircase that led upstairs. She wondered if Donald would come down and catch the mysterious stranger in their house.

"Now isn't a good time, Mrs. Prescott. My husband is upstairs in the bedroom and he hasn't been feeling well lately. He—"

"Your husband is asleep Barbara," Maria interrupted the concerned wife. "He doesn't have a choice. It's his time to snooze. Just let me look around the house and get a better understanding of what we are dealing with here, all right? I won't disturb your husband."

"I don't understand." Barbara shook her head. "How could you possibly know that my husband is asleep? Why would he have no choice?"

Maria pressed her right index finger against Barbara's lips and brought her peace.

"No more questions child. I grow tired from your lack of confidence in my abilities. Now stay here, as I said, and let me help you." She stared deeply into Barbara's eyes.

"Fine." Barbara angrily surrendered to the stranger's commands and walked to the living room where she sat on the sofa and crossed her legs. Misty woke and hurried to her mistress's side for affection.

Maria Prescott walked into the downstairs bathroom and spent very little time inside of it before exiting and continuing down the hallway toward

Barbara's office. She entered the room and began a conversation with herself. Her words were muffled and Barbara was unable to make them out, even after turning her ear toward the sounds for more clarity. After only three minutes, Maria exited the office and walked to the end of the hall, where she stood in the living room and scanned the area, avoiding eye contact with Barbara. Nodding her head, ever so delicately, the strange, thickset woman turned and ascended the staircase, one step at a time. It took her a good two minutes to reach the top, holding tightly to the banister the entire way up. The wide hole in the wood panelling, from Mary's accident, had been repaired by a contractor a few weeks earlier, but Maria made a point of stopping briefly on the stairs and staring at the wall that had been previously damaged. She turned into Amanda's bedroom then, and spent a considerable amount of time inside. The muted sound of the woman's deep voice resonated from within. Barbara was aware that the woman was asking questions and pausing in between them for responses that never seemed to come. But the woman's pattern of speech led Barbara to believe that, for some reason, a response *was* being offered.

The woman left Amanda's room and stood facing the master bedroom, where Donald was presumably sleeping. She didn't enter it, but continued down the hallway instead. Barbara could hear her weighty footsteps in the upstairs bathroom, and eventually in Mary's room.

The clock on the wall now read 2:15 p.m. and Barbara knew that she would soon have to pick up the two girls from school. She became slightly agitated and squirmed on the chesterfield, crossing her right leg over her left, and then her left over her right, repeatedly. Maria was upstairs for quite some time. Barbara knew that she would have investigated Richard's bedroom by now, but the sound of her shallow voice was no longer obvious. After twelve minutes upstairs, Maria descended the staircase, one step at a time, holding the banister tightly, and stopped at the bottom. Barbara stood up and spoke out to her.

"Mrs. Prescott, I have to pick up my children from school soon. Don't you think that I should let my husband know that you are here? He may be able to assist you. He's had many experiences here in the house, as well."

"No!" Maria reprimanded the frightened woman. "Your husband, Donald, is extremely ill, Barbara. He should not be disturbed, do you understand? The less he is provoked, the better. At least until I am able to repair things for you. That's important!" She raised her voice. "Don't provoke him right now Barbara, and tell your children the same. Donald is in a very precarious position right now. Do not provoke him!" Maria continued toward the basement door. As she reached out to the handle, she turned and glared sternly toward the living-room area again, commanding Barbara to heed her words. "If you want me to fix this, Barbara, do not provoke your husband. That wouldn't be a wise idea … at all." She opened the door and headed down the stairs.

Barbara looked at the wall clock again and then glanced up the staircase toward the master bedroom door. She rocked her body back and forth, and then sat again to calm her nerves. Maria spent another eight minutes in the seclusion of the dreary, dark basement. Now Barbara could hear her husband stirring upstairs and feared him coming down to confront the stranger in their house. Barbara sat up and started walking toward the basement as the door swung open and Maria returned to the main level.

"Don't forget what I told you." She looked straight at Barbara. "Your house is very contaminated, and it's really quite fascinating. I know about the claims and the horror that took place here, Barbara. Your house was one of my special projects you know." She smiled, exposing her crooked yellow teeth. "I really had no idea that this house contained an evil though. This is a surprise to me."

"What do you mean?" Barbara asked. "What evil

are you referring to?"

Maria Prescott started walking toward the front entrance and slipped on her sandals.

"You have a demon here in your house, Barbara."

"A what?!" exclaimed Barbara. "A demon? What are you talking about?"

Mrs. Prescott stopped and turned after opening up the wooden door. "There are two different energy sources here. Three, if you were to count yourselves. But it's the demon that you fear, Barbara. It's that evil that we need to dispose of. The sooner the better too." She stepped outside.

"Where are you going?" Barbara asked, suddenly terrified. "Please don't leave now. I thought you were going to fix this for us! What are we supposed to do about this now, Mrs. Prescott?"

"Patience Barbara!" Maria snapped back at the frantic Sterling woman. "You have to be patient. Do not provoke him; do you understand? I will come back. Let me figure things out for you and I'll be back."

Maria walked out of the house and down the front-entrance stairs, waddling her way to her green Volkswagen Beetle. As she opened the car door, she slowly turned back to the house where Barbara stood rigid on the front step.

"Do not provoke him, Barbara! Soon your family will be whole again." The woman got into the car (testing the small vehicle's shocks as they compressed fully), started it up, and proceeded to drive backwards down the long, unpaved driveway. Barbara watched and was suddenly interrupted by a terrifying, but familiar voice.

"And who was that?" Donald stood in the living room watching the car as it turned onto the main street. "What did they want?" He spoke to her rather slowly, jealousy resonating through his aura. He stepped closer to his wife and ground his teeth.

Barbara was afraid. She didn't know how to answer her husband, who had appeared in the living-room area shirtless and wearing only his lemon yellow briefs. She closed the front door and watched her husband making his way toward her one short step at a time. Uncertain of his reaction, Barbara tensed up and prepared herself in a defensive posture.

"Who was that, I asked you? Can you not hear me?" His temper rose.

"It was just the Avon lady, Donald. She was trying to sell me some make-up. I told her that I didn't need any, but she insisted that I try her new fragrance."

Donald walked in close to Barbara and leaned over, within mere inches, to smell her neck. Barbara held her breath and prayed to herself for amnesty from her husband's volatile and easily triggered temperament. After taking several deep breaths through his nose, he reacted and lurched back.

"It smells like sage," he said. "I can smell it all over the place in here. Even upstairs for God's sake. I sure in the hell hope that you didn't buy any of that shit. We don't need to be spending our money on garbage like that. Tell me that you didn't buy any." Donald looked angrily into his wife's eyes. "When are you going to learn that money doesn't grow on trees? We can't exactly afford to live in the lap of luxury, if you're blowing our money on shit like that, now can we?"

"N-no," Barbara was quick to say. "I didn't like it either. I sent her on her way. She's gone now and I didn't buy anything. I promise."

Donald continued to stare at Barbara with a scowl on his worn face. The situation quickly became uncomfortable and critical in Barbara's mind.

Just then, the telephone rang. The high-pitched sound carved through the tension in the room and jolted both of the Sterling adults from their animosities. Donald retreated and headed down to the basement, while Barbara walked to the kitchen and grabbed the receiver.

"Hello?" she asked meekly.

"Hello, Mrs. Sterling. This is Doctor Collins at Mercy General Hospital." The doctor had a tone in his voice that was unfamiliar to Barbara. It was peaceful and contained a level of hope. "I have some great news, for once, Mrs. Sterling. Richard, as you know, is talking. He is asking for you. His speech is improving and he's getting stronger with each hour that passes."

"That is fantastic news, Doctor Collins! When can we bring him home?" Barbara had tears in her eyes from yet another emotional day. The doctor, on the other end of the phone, announced the words that Barbara had waited on for over two years.

"I am going to recommend that Richard be discharged from the hospital tomorrow, Mrs. Sterling. He is ready, and I think that you are too. Are you ready for Richard's return, Mrs. Sterling? I'm sure that Donald will be excited for his arrival … and the girls?"

"Oh yes," Barbara turned and looked at the entrance to the kitchen, focusing her attention and hearing toward the door leading to the basement. She wanted to ensure that Donald hadn't snuck up behind her. "They will be ecstatic to hear the news. I have to pick them up from school now and then I'll come by the hospital to see Richard and talk to you—"

"Mrs. Sterling?" The doctor was quick to cut into the conversation. "Richard is sleeping right now and I need to step out to a house call down by the old mine road. Why don't you take this time to prepare your house for your son's arrival and spend some time with your loving family, discussing the ways that you can make his return a special one?"

"Oh, okay," Barbara agreed, "If that's what you feel is best." She smiled from ear to ear, which she perceived as a rare feeling lately. "You are the doctor, after all."

Barbara hung up the phone, vibrating—overjoyed by the doctor's news. She paced back and forth for a moment in the kitchen, before walking around to the closed basement door, where she stopped abruptly. After a brief thought process, Barbara walked away, grabbed the van's keys, and slipped on her shoes, leaving to pick up her girls from school.

That evening was a festive one for most of the Sterling family. Barbara and the girls jogged around the living room, chasing Misty, who was in a playful mood. Barbara had picked up some balloons and a cake, along with a huge banner that read *"Welcome Home."* The females of the family decorated the living space and joyfully prepared for their brother and son to return home. Donald sat on the chair and watched intently. His face remained emotionless, but he presented no immediate danger to his family and just sat, disengaged and lost. By 9:00 p.m., the girls gave their father a hug and he, in turn, wrapped his arms around them individually. He didn't speak to them though; he wouldn't even make the effort. They headed upstairs and prepared for bed. Tomorrow was going to be a fantastic day! Their brother was finally going to be home and they were given permission from their teachers to miss school in order to celebrate. It had been a request from Barbara when she picked them up from school earlier. After twenty minutes, the girls had likely fallen asleep and Barbara swiftly and efficiently tidied up before looking over to Donald.

"I'm going to bed, Donald." She hesitated and a lump developed in her throat. "It … it sure would be nice if you joined me. We don't have to stop celebrating, if you really don't want to."

She walked to her husband's chair and carefully went down on her knees in front of him, reaching over and grabbing his hand, placing it on her breast over top of her blouse. She then took her left hand and slid it up Donald's thigh, where it stopped after meeting his fortification. She smiled brightly at him and her eyes became glassy and hopeful. Barbara moved her body closer to her lost husband and kissed him, passionately, on the lips. Donald looked at his wife and left his hand where she had placed it. He looked into her eyes and did show some genuine emotion, but struggled to maintain the clarity of his current reality. He removed his clasp from his wife's breast and clutched her hand in his own, and stood up, pulling her closer to his height. Barbara beamed and embraced Donald in a loving hug. The two then walked, hand in hand, up the staircase and into to their bedroom, where they closed the door behind them.

By midnight, the house was quiet. The Sterling family slept. Misty lay by the fireplace and napped. The clock's second hand made a distinct ticking sound that made it vibrate as it hung. The kitchen's light bulb began turning on and off and the sound of the light switch was evident, as it clicked back and forth. Misty woke up and looked toward the kitchen. She started growling and stood up, walking toward the kitchen. The chair in the living room slid sideways and blocked her direct path. She whimpered and jumped back in fear. A magazine that was on the side table beside the chair landed on the floor. The dog watched in amazement as the pages started to turn. One by one, the pages rapidly flipped over top of one another until the magazine was finally closed once again. Misty let out a yelp and quickly ran up the staircase. Footsteps resonated on the hardwood floor downstairs, but the Sterling family remained oblivious to the noises and activity that was taking place below them. Unfortunately, the joyous preparations for Richard's gleeful return were, apparently, still in progress.

14

The Perils of a Triumphant Homecoming

September 13, 1979

At 6:30 in the morning, an excited Mary Sterling came out of her room and used the washroom. Her adrenaline outweighed her sleepiness, in anticipation of her brother's return and the delight of his well-being, which she greatly missed. She quickly washed her hands clean and exited the washroom, starting downstairs to enjoy a glass of milk. Her hungry canine friend, Misty, followed at her heels and Mary ensured that, this time, she grabbed on tightly to the banister, as she had done ever since her painful accident. By the third stair down, through the faded light that entered the room from the picture window, Mary encountered an alarming sight. She looked down at the furniture in the living room, which had all been turned upside down or knocked over. Even the chesterfield was leaning on its face. The corner lamp was broken, shattered on the floor, and had been pulled from its wall plug. The girl and her pet dog froze on the stairs and Mary became increasingly more frightened as the seconds passed. She turned around quickly and headed back to the upper floor with Misty in tow. Mary knocked sharply on her parents' bedroom door.

"Mom, Dad, wake up! Someone has been in the house. I think we've been robbed!" Mary listened as her parents rustled around in the room, and after ten seconds Barbara opened the door tying her robe around her waist.

"Mary, what are you going on about?" There was panic in her voice, which was the direct result of her daughter's declaration. "What do you mean someone's been in the house?"

Mary turned and pointed down the stairs as Barbara's eyes caught the chaotic mess beneath her. Amanda came out of her room and followed her family's stares.

"What happened, Mommy?" Amanda was confounded. "How come the chairs are upside down?"

Barbara made her way down the staircase, very aware of her immediate surroundings, and proceeded with caution. The two girls and Misty followed closely behind as Donald exited the bedroom and was immobilized at the threshold, watching his girls drop away from him to the main level. The balloons that they had decorated with the night before had been ripped from the chairs. Some lay on the floor while others had popped. The welcome home banner above the mantel was hanging by a single corner, draped in front of the fireplace. Barbara glanced timidly up the stairs to her husband, who she'd spent intimate moments with the night before. He peered down and presented a look of complete innocence. Barbara walked to the base of the staircase as the girls began tidying up.

"Donald, please tell me that you didn't do this. Tell me that you didn't wake in the night and cause this disarray." She feared his response.

Donald lowered his head and slowly shook it back and forth. His face projected disappointment.

"No Barbara. N-no, I really didn't do it." He walked backwards, keeping his eyes on his wife, and then re-entered the bedroom and he closed the door.

Riddled with guilt, Barbara turned her attention back to her daughters. She looked out the window and walked through the entire house, looking for any forced entry or clues to an invasion. Perhaps the intruder was still in the house. The disrupted living area had been ransacked without raising any alarm at all, nothing that had woken up her family at least. Barbara looked into her office and the washroom before opening the basement door and flicking on the light. She listened for a moment at the top of the stairs and gained confidence that no one was in the house who shouldn't be. *At least no one alive*, she thought to herself. Once realizing that there was no indication of an unlawful entry, Barbara walked back to the living room to assist her two daughters with the clean up.

"Okay girls, can you give me a hand and we'll get this furniture back on its legs? The chesterfield and the love-seat are really heavy." Barbara and Mary grabbed a side of the sofa and struggled as they flipped it back to its natural position. Barbara continued to address her two daughters as they all worked. "Today, we pick up Richard from the hospital. I'm so excited. I bet that you are too!"

Amanda looked up and nodded to her mother with a huge grin on her face. Her young innocence shone through her. Mary, on the other hand, had more on her mind.

"How did the furniture get like this, Mom? Aren't you a little bit worried about how this happened?"

"Of course I am, Mary, but there's no reason to let it ruin Rich's homecoming. We'll clean it up and worry about it later, okay?" Barbara looked up the stairs to ensure that the coast was clear and whispered to her middle child. "You know your father is not feeling well. This was, more than likely, caused by him. Dad has been angry. You know that honey, and we are trying to work our way through it. Don't ruin this for your brother, Mary." She leaned over and spoke even softer. "And don't scare your little sister, okay? Please, today is going to be a good day."

Mary was confused and twisted her face in disbelief at her mother's opinion. The three of them continued putting the living area back in order and salvaged as many of the party decorations as they possibly could. Eventually the three Sterling girls had returned the large family room back to its original state, before retiring to the kitchen and dining-room area for some breakfast.

By 8:43 a.m., the Sterling girls had cleaned up the kitchen and prepared for their exciting trip to the hospital to pick up their Richard, after two long years, and bring him home. Donald knew it too. Somewhere, deep inside of his soul, he was able to grasp the importance of his son's recovery, but was unable to demonstrate his true glee. He stood at the side entrance, for fifteen minutes, waiting patiently for the rest of his family.

The Sterlings all crammed into their bright red van

and drove to Mercy Hospital. It was Barbara behind the wheel. Donald would choose the shotgun position more often lately, without question. They arrived and flooded out of the van at 9:20 a.m., hurrying themselves inside with Donald bringing up the rear. Mary held on to a bright yellow helium balloon that had survived the apparent vandalism in their living room the previous night and the entire family entered Richard's hospital room, where he sat on the edge of his bed. His suitcases were packed and he had a pair of crutches, since his walking technique had been impeded by his long, horizontal rest. He beamed with happiness and it was a glorious sight for the Sterling family.

"H-hi mom! Hi guys," Richard looked to his father. "Hi Dad ... h-how are you doing?" Donald nodded his head, but showed no joy for his son.

"Hi Rich," Barbara ran over to give her son a big hug. "We missed you so much. You're talking better today. Do you feel better now, Rich?" Mary and Amanda joined in on the hugs, but Richard's happy mood began to change. All he could concentrate on was his father's demeanour.

"I ... I feel really great, Mom. I ... th-think that I'm ready to come home n-now. The doctor even said that I could." He continued looking at his father, who stared blankly back at him.

Barbara noticed her son's eye direction and looked

back to Donald in disappointment.

"Donald, don't you want to give Rich a big hug? He sure would like that." Donald didn't budge. He remained sad and disheartened, but his bottom lip began to quiver.

"Mom, it's … okay," Richard said, disillusioned. "If Dad … d-doesn't want to give me … a hug, it's okay. Maybe he's just a little e-emotional that I'm awake … now."

The Sterling family glared at Donald and an uncomfortable numbness filled the air. Donald gradually shuffled to Richard's bedside and extended his arms around him. Richard slowly, but weakly, returned the hug. His head rested upon his father's heaving chest and a tear trickled down his cheek as he listened to his sporadic heartbeat. As the family looked on with smiles, the conflicted man spoke.

"I'm glad you are feeling better, Richard. Everybody has missed you. Even the dog, I think." The girls all let out small instinctive chuckles to lighten the mood. Father and son continued to lovingly embrace and there was a short pause before Donald continued on.

"I'm going to give you some advice, okay Richard?" the two severed their encirclement and Donald looked his son in the eyes, putting his hand on Richard's greasy, messy long hair. "I suggest that you don't hate being in the house. I wouldn't tell the house that you hate it there and that it should go to hell. I don't think that would be a good idea if you did that anymore." Donald stared at his son with authority and an air of an immense intimidation. "I think it's best if you apologize to the house when we get back home; don't you think?"

The entire family held their breath and pondered why the man of the family would make such bold and misguided statements. Richard carefully observed his father's scowl and hesitated, looking for an answer. As he tried to speak, he was interrupted by his sweet and naive youngest sister, who stepped toward her father.

"What do you mean, Daddy?" asked Amanda, but she was ignored by all.

"Oh … okay Dad, I … won't do that anymore. I'm really sorry." Richard knew that he *had* proclaimed his father's exact words privately in the house before his accident. There would be no way, though, for his dad to know what he had said. That would be impossible. He had been alone in his room. His father must have been listening from outside the door. But then again, he *was* yelling quite loudly though … so he must have heard him. That would, most certainly, be the only reasonable explanation.

Donald patted his son on the head and looked over to his wife with a slight smile that seemed to crack his cheeks and looked unnatural. As the girls swarmed

Richard and moved in for another hug from their brother, Barbara grabbed some of Richard's clothing and his toiletry bag before moving toward the door.

"Well, what do you say we get out of here? I'm sure that we have some papers to sign before we go. Mary, can you grab that bag for me? I know that your Misty girl is very excited to see you too, Rich."

Richard hobbled to his feet and placed his crutches under his armpits. The family left the hospital room, together, for the first time in two years and the situation seemed surreal to everyone, including the hospital's regular staff, who had presented Richard with a huge bouquet of flowers before his departure. The Sterling family finally left the hospital after packing up and made their way home—a complete, but still broken, clan.

The side door to the Sterlings' troubled house opened at 9:49 on that warm, bright Thursday morning. Misty quickly came running from the backyard, where she had been hunting down insects in the long autumn grass. She paid special attention to Richard, jumping up on him and gently licking his warm face as he knelt down to her. Barbara, Richard, and the two girls joked and laughed as they entered the property. It was as if Richard was arriving at the house for the first time and a bright smile appeared.

Unfortunately, there was an immediate sensation of

fear and horror once inside. The air in the old house was cold and thick. Barbara looked down the hallway and toward the living room. She took three quick steps forward and let out a screech. The Sterling family stopped where they stood, orienting themselves with the reality of the situation and moving forward to join Barbara in her disbelief. The living room had been vandalized again! It was worse than before. The chesterfield was flung up against the fireplace and a leg on one of the chairs had been broken clean off. The remaining decorations had been shredded, including the banner, and lay in a pile on the hardwood floor. Photos of the family had been flung across the room and shattered against the walls. It was clear that someone had been in the house, but who? Donald stood at the entrance to the family area and appeared content. The rest of the family, including Richard, were terrified and couldn't relate to the possibility of an intruder who could possibly have caused such damage in the short period of time that the Sterlings were away. And there was no forced entry again. Richard laid his crutches against the wall and grabbed a side table, turning it upright.

"Who ... who did this, Mom? Why w-would someone come in the ... house and do something ... crazy like this?" There was a level of controlled panic in his voice.

"I don't think anybody came in to the house, Rich,"

Barbara looked over to Donald. "I think whoever did this has been here all along." Donald glared back in reaction to his wife's bold words. "I think that whatever did this, for the second time today, by the way, doesn't want us to be here. Your dad knows who it is, don't you?" She yearned for his sanity.

"What ... w-what is that supposed to mean, Mom?" Richard asked for clarification. "This ... this is the second time that this has happened? It ... it already happened today? Is that what ... what you said?" Richard paused. "M-Mom is right. There ... is someone here ... b-but you have it all wrong." Richard glanced to his father. "I ... told you! There are ... bad things here. I told you all, didn't I? But you're ... w-wrong about what's ... h-here. You're all wrong." Richard started to breathe heavily and anger washed through his body. Donald stared at his son and scowled at his words.

"I think you should go upstairs to your room, Richard, that's what I think." Donald was persistent.

"What in God's name are you talking about, Donald?" Barbara interjected. "Our son has just come back home after two years of being in a coma! You're sending him to his room? He's 17 years old now for God's sake." Barbara couldn't believe her man could be so cold hearted. Donald began to fume. He walked over to the side table that Richard had just placed upright, picked it up, and threw it forcefully across the living room, where it smashed against the hall's partition.

"I said go to your room!" he screamed at the top of his lungs. "Now!" Misty ran to the top floor in fear, Amanda immediately began to cry, and Mary retreated to the far corner of the living room, fearing her father's next moves. After lowering his head in disgust, Richard took his crutches and limped up the stairs to his bedroom. Barbara stared at Donald and was clearly terrified, but after a few deep breaths, the man walked away and escaped into the basement, closing the door behind him.

The joy that was anticipated for the day was short lived. Barbara and the girls were recreating their early morning clean-up of the living-room area and attempted to build positivity around their family. Something remained out of place, besides the personal property, though. The mental stability of the entire clan was in extreme jeopardy. Time might have finally run out, once and for all, for the Sterling family and it seemed that the house itself was in control of winding the watch.

15
Confessions from the Other Side

September 16, 1979

By Sunday, Richard was walking without his crutches and only had a minor limp when he moved. His speech was now one hundred percent and he began to orientate himself with his memorable but unfamiliar surroundings. Having missed so much school, Barbara Sterling arranged for her son to take homeschooling for the calendar year and catch up the best that he could. Richard didn't speak like the average 17- year-old boy though. His voice had transformed through the natural means of puberty, but his educational level had stalled and he spoke and acted like a normal boy two years younger, in spite of an undeniable maturity he showed in certain regards. He looked down the staircase at his mother, who was sitting on the love-seat watching her programming on the twenty-four inch, wood-encased, colour television, which sat in the corner near the fireplace and large picture window. She looked dishevelled and confused. He went downstairs to talk to his mom and clear some things up once and for all. It was time that they were all told the mandatory and definitive truths surrounding their dire situation.

Much to Barbara's surprise, Donald had vacated the house in the early morning with his camera equipment, and left a note which read, "*Shooting today … Donald.*" This would be the first time in weeks that he took the initiative to provide for his family. *Perhaps*, Barbara thought, *the tides are changing.* The girls played in the backyard with Misty, awaiting their brother's arrival, as he had promised them that he would push them on the tire swing.

Richard arrived at the bottom of the stairs and sat with his mother on the love-seat. He wore a white, collared dress shirt and a pair of black, cotton dress pants that needed the hem taken down fully to cover the boy's ankles. He had certainly grown taller and Barbara could count every extra inch as a nearly tragic loss in her own mind. She reached over and gave her son a tight and loving hug.

"Hi Rich. How are you doing today? It looks to me like you're getting better ... stronger even. I'm so proud of you Richard, and I love you so much. You really have no idea."

"I know you do, Mom. I love you too. I think that I'm feeling pretty good." Richard broke the embrace with his mother. "Mom? I really need to tell you some stuff that happened when I was in the hospital okay?" He hesitated, until Barbara, whose expression showed concern, nodded.

"Sure Rich, you can tell me anything. Did something happen in the hospital that I should maybe know about?" She glanced around the living space. "That *we* should know about?"

Richard slipped back into the plush love-seat to be more comfortable.

"Mom, the bad things that are happening here are not exactly what you and Dad think."

"What do you mean by 'exactly'?"

"When I was in the hospital and asleep, I was visited by four people."

Barbara was puzzled. She stared into her son's iron gaze and squinted her eyes.

"Four people ... what are you taking about, Rich?"

"I was visited by four people. Some together and some alone. They spoke right to me, Mom. They told me most of the story, and now I know."

Barbara recoiled her slender body. She wrinkled her forehead and didn't believe her son.

"You must have been dreaming, Richard. These things don't just happen you know." But then she remembered the night when she saw the woman in the white nightgown who directed her to the basement door and her son's tragic emergency. She thought of the night that she saw the vision of Richard, as a younger boy, on her bedroom ceiling and the voices coming from Amanda's room. After a pause and sensing that Richard was dejected, Barbara realized that she had become very contradictory and changed her direction quickly. "I'm so sorry, Rich ... I'm listening honey. Please go on."

"Mom, our home was owned by the Murphy family. The mean kids at school talked about this house and the evil presence inside of it." He looked around. "The evil presence that surrounds us every day. Their father built the house in the early nineteen hundreds and horrible things have happened here. Really, really bad things Mom."

Barbara remembered the research that Donald had done and his vital findings, which associated the Murphy family to Richard's accident, and it was easy for her to recall that he had blamed a man named Charles for the whole ordeal. Barbara was afraid to ask, as she already knew the answer.

"What sort of bad things, Rich?" she asked, sheepishly. "Who told you this?"

Richard paused and placed his hand on his mother's arm to support her next reaction. He took a deep breath and immediately sent his mother's shattered heart racing with his blood-curdling response.

"The Murphy family came to visit me in the hospital mom. A nice, but defeated-looking woman named Marion came with her little daughter, whose name was Dorothy. She was beautiful, Mom. She had long hair and it reached to the middle of her back. It was even longer than Amanda's hair. And Dorothy walked with a slight limp. She never told me why, but I think she was sick, like me, when she was alive."

Barbara's mouth drooped open and her mind slowly began to rearrange a great number of puzzle pieces. She smiled sadly as tears appeared in her eyes.

"Go on sweetheart, please." She couldn't hold back her emotions any longer and started to weep in front of her son.

"They told me some real things, Mom. They told me that they live here … even today, and that I wasn't supposed to be afraid. They told me that they were trapped and when I asked them why, they said it was because of the evil that is in the house."

The horrified mother reached up and wiped away

her tears as she became compelled to learn more.

"I asked them what the evil was, but they told me that they weren't allowed to tell me." He shifted his position on the love-seat as the intense conversation was interrupted by the girls barging in through the side door.

"Richard, what's taking you so long? Why aren't you coming outside? We've both been waiting forever!" The two girls ran into the living room and knew that they had interrupted a serious and complicated conversation.

"I'll be there in a minute, I swear," Richard assured his sisters. "I'm just telling Mom how I'm feeling, because she asked and we're just talking, that's all. I'll be there as soon as I can."

"We are having a chat for a minute, okay girls?" Barbara added. "Go back out and play ... Rich will come and join you outside soon."

The girls were satisfied and ran back outside to the big oak tree in the corner of the yard. After a brief pause, Richard looked back at his awaiting mother and continued with his frightening story.

"I was also visited by another person. He was a very big man and his name was Charles."

Barbara immediately got a lump in her throat, and she began to perspire.

Richard continued, "Charles was Dorothy's father. He was married to Marion, but they never visited me at the same time. I don't know why. Charles had a big opening in his head, Mom. He scared me at first, but then we talked and I'm not scared of him anymore." He said that they live, as undead, in this house, but made sure to tell me, over and over again, that they live here in a completely different realm than the evil one. He also told me that he couldn't tell me who he was, because this evil ghost can really hurt them and he does on a regular basis."

Barbara looked stunned and began to wring her hands together, cracking her knuckles in the process.

"Oh my goodness, Richard, what do we do? How do we fight something like that? We need to find a way to get rid of the evil presence in our house. How do we do that?"

"*We* can't do anything, Mom. They are all trapped here. Charles, Marion, and Dorothy want to leave, but they're trapped here. The evil is trapped here too. It caused my accident and Charles told me that it made him hurt his family. When they died, Charles says the evil one was responsible. It killed them all, including Charles. The evil one killed Charles too."

Barbara Sterling calculated her thoughts and squinted while grabbing Richard's hands. She realized that her son had experienced much more than she had comprehended.

"Oh, Richard, so the fourth person to visit you was

this evil one? Oh my God, that must have been so frightening for you."

Richard shook his head. "No, mom, it wasn't the evil one who visited me. I've never even met it ... *him*, I mean. Charles talked about it as a 'him'. Most of us living people can't see him, but he's here. Only a small minority of the living can see him. The Murphy family can see him though, Mom. I don't think we can, but *they* sure can. They can't communicate with the evil though. They try, but he doesn't hear them and then he hurts them. He hurts them all the time."

"Well then, who was your fourth visitor, son?"

Richard tightened the grip on his mother's hands. "He was a funny fellow, Mom. He said that he was really new to the whole *'undead'* world and that he didn't live in our house anymore. He lived nearby, but not in our house now. He's trapped too, Mom, and he said that he doesn't like the evil one at all. He told me that this evil one framed him, years back, and caused a really bad accident that took a boy's life. He told me his name was Jack, and he only visited me once. He was judged as an evil person while he was alive Mom, so when he died ... I think it was just last year ... he told me that he was placed into the same realm as the evil one. Jack says that he steers clear of the evil one though. He doesn't go near him, because he's very afraid."

Barbara leaned over and gave her son another hug,

almost preventing him from confessing more. She rose from the love-seat and walked to the vast picture window, staring out at the front trees.

"Mom? The evil one is the reason I got sick. He's the reason I had my accident, and he's the reason that dad is so sick too. I saw his pain. I saw your pain too. I wanted to give you a hug, but I couldn't. I did see you though, Mom. You were so sad and it made me want to come to you."

"Really. Okay," Barbara chuckled uncomfortably, "and how exactly could you see us, Rich?"

"I saw it from right there." He joined his mother at the window. "I saw it from right there on the porch bench, with Charles. He brought me here and we sat right there." He pointed down at the wooden bench outside. "Charles comes here all the time, Mom. That's what he told me."

They both watched as Donald's red van pulled off of the street and onto the long driveway. Barbara pulled her body away from the gaping window, but Richard stood his ground and stared out toward his father as he drove past his sightline. He turned his head and offered some advice.

"Don't be afraid of Dad, Mom. He won't hurt you, if you just leave him alone. He doesn't want to be provoked. You shouldn't provoke him, Mom." Barbara knew that she had heard this before.

Richard strolled to the far end of the living room as Donald parked the van.

"Well, I better get outside before Mary kills me." The two looked at each other uncomfortably for a moment and then Donald entered through the side door. Richard walked past him on his way out and they shared a glance. "Hi Dad." He didn't make eye contact with his father. "I'm going outside with Mary and Amanda. Bye." Donald quickly responded by nodding his head as his son exited. He paused for a moment while looking back at the door.

Donald Sterling threw his tan camera bag on the floor beside the basement door and walked into the living room, where Barbara was standing in the middle of the large area rug. He looked at his wife with an emotionless stare while pushing his glasses up closer to his face.

"What was that all about?" he asked. "What were you two talking about? I feel that I've walked into your secret."

She found it quite difficult to speak her mind. "Richard was telling me that he had visitors while he was in the hospital. They're similar stories to what you had told me, after your research at the library. I think that you may be wrong about what you think is happening, Donald. There seems to be more to the sto—"

"Oh, I see," Donald interrupted, "This is all about

me again, is it? The fact that I never visited Richard at the hospital as much as you did? Is that what this is about?" He became infuriated and clenched his fists, rearing up to attack once again.

"No," Barbara defended herself, "it wasn't about you!" He stopped and took a step back. "He told me the exact same thing that you did about the Murphys, Donald! He said that there is an evil one and it made him and you sick. You're sick, Donald! You're sick because of this 'evil one.' And the others are lost. They are lost and just want to leave, but they can't because they're trapped. Richard was visited by the Murphy family, Donald. I heard it with my own ears. And that explains so much, Donald, don't you think?"

Donald took a step toward his wife and leaned over to address her.

"You're fucking kidding me, right?" Barbara's eyes grew large once more. "The kid was in a coma, Barbara. He was in a God damn coma. You know that he didn't have any visitors. He's a good story teller though." He backed down and gave Barbara more space.

"No Donald, he told me and it all makes sense. Think about it, Donald. Think about it. It all makes sense now. All of th—" Donald quickly lifted his hand to Barbara's face and pointed his large index finger straight between her eyes, stopping her mid-sentence.

"I think it's a creative story. Maybe you can write

about it someday." He cracked the largest smile that Barbara had seen in months. "Why don't you just leave it alone, Barbara? Just forget about it. Richard is back now and all is good in the world." He spoke very delicately and nodded his head. "Just leave it now, understand?"

Barbara was unable to respond and simply watched as her husband strolled away from her and headed upstairs, disappearing into the master bedroom. Barbara reached up and threw her hair back out of her eyes, shuffling her feet and contemplating her next move.

Amanda opened up the side door and walked into the living room where her mother stood. She grabbed at her mother's hand and glanced up at her as Barbara met her distraught eyes. She had an agitated look on her face and spoke slowly and calmly, appearing perplexed and in need of an explanation.

"Mommy, I saw the man in the tree again. He tried to scare me again, so I showed Richard. He saw that the man was there too, and you know what he told me? Richard told me to stay away from the man in the tree, because he is the 'evil one.' Then Richard walked away from me after that. I don't know what he means, Mommy. Why does he have to call the man in the tree 'the evil one?' He doesn't look very evil to me. He doesn't even look scary to me, Mommy. He kind of looks like he's just dead ... most of the time."

16
Dorothy's Tour

October 29, 1979

It was two days before Halloween. Activity in and around the Sterlings' home seemed to subside a bit. Even Donald seemed to be slowly coming around. He would try to join his family for his meals and was taking more photographs, spending only productive hours in the basement. Richard had healed. He was joyful again and accepted the reality of what the house offered. He continued his home schooling and showed some great progress as his brain was able to comprehend what he had missed in the past two years. Amanda and Mary continued excelling with their schoolwork and reports from teachers offered little criticism. In fact, Mary had been revered by her peers, becoming very popular, and was always the first considered for assisting the teachers with important curriculum projects.

There had been no word from the mysterious medium who had visited the previous month. Barbara surrendered to the fact that the woman was simply a crazy, freelance psychic who wanted to proclaim her research on the property. She promised that she would help out and maybe she had. After all, there didn't seem to be any need for panic in their current day-to-day lives.

The day was a Monday and it was late in the evening, about 11:15 p.m. The weather outside was frigid and the mornings began to display frost on the overgrown grass outside. The two young girls were asleep, as they had school the next day, and Richard slept too. He would need to study in the morning and continue improving. Donald retired the earliest and had already been sleeping for three hours. Barbara left the office with Misty following behind her. She had spent a good portion of the day working on her new project. Her previous work had been sent to her publisher only weeks before, but there had been no word yet. A new inspiration ignited her creative juices and it was a result of their current situation, so she dove deep into a new ambitious novel, which was gaining impressive progress.

Barbara undressed and slipped on some warm, purple-striped flannel pyjamas before joining her husband in bed. She shuffled over and cuddled up, spooning with Donald, who lay on his side in the fetal position. After comfortably falling asleep, Barbara dreamt of a faraway dwelling. Alone and disoriented, she met up with a little girl in a fantasy land that was surrounded by clouds and beams of light. Barbara walked for miles with the little girl, who guided her through a series of endless tunnels and crevices. She tossed and turned as she dreamed and her eyes moved under her lids while she let out the occasional moan.

At three in the morning Barbara awoke as her bladder forced her to go and relieve herself. She got out of bed, slipped on her slippers, and headed to the washroom across the hall. Barbara sat on the toilet with sleep closing her eyes and took care of her business. She began to hear a faint noise from the hallway outside. It was electrical in tone—a solid buzzing that seemed to intensify as she washed her hands. She exited from the washroom and turned toward Amanda's room, where she saw a shining ball of light directly in front of her youngest daughter's door. It was obvious that this ball of intense energy was the source of the electrical buzz she had clearly heard while in the bathroom. The sphere of light hummed and vibrated, but not loud enough to wake the rest of the family. All at once, the light got brighter and grew larger in size. Barbara stood her ground and watched in pure amazement. The shining anomaly expanded to the size and shape of a small human being. As the light began to dim, Barbara stared at a child, no more than 5 or 6 years old, who was floating in front of her. She had no legs or feet, but resonated a beautiful smile and aura. She wore a little white nightgown and had noticeable dark black rings underneath her eyes. Her blonde hair flowed down to one side, propelled by an unseen force. Barbara knew that the little girl who faced her was none other than Dorothy Murphy. The little girl stretched out her right arm toward Barbara.

"Come with me," she said. *"I want to show you something."*

Barbara reached out her shaking hand to the small child without question or hesitation. Her fingers crackled and tingled as they met the stinging energy of the little girl's appendage. Her head began to spin and she felt as if she was being warped or transformed into an alternate realm of existence. Barbara closed her eyes tightly and sensed, with astonishment, that her body remained completely level and balanced, even though her brain told her that she was wildly twirling. The sensation lasted only nine seconds, but to Barbara, it seemed like hours.

Once the pounding jackhammering distraction within her head subsided, Barbara opened her eyes to an amazing and magical sight. She viewed her surroundings in black and white, scanning the hallway and doors. Rubbing her eyes, Barbara shook her head and looked again, but the eerie colourless emptiness still existed. It was as if she was watching her parents' television as a young child, but this time, she was the star of the show. Barbara looked down and to her left. The little girl was still standing beside her. The young child stared toward Amanda's bedroom with an intensity in her dark and sunken eyes. She turned and looked up at Barbara before pointing at her daughter's bedroom door, and then began to move toward it. When she reached the doorway, the small child pivoted and looked back to Barbara, reaching her hand out, just as before.

Barbara couldn't help herself. She shuffled her slippers toward the girl standing in front of Amanda's room and reached out to take her hand once again. The little girl refused Barbara's gesture, and instead, pointed at Amanda's bedroom door with a blank expression. Barbara felt compelled to enter the room, and as she reached out to turn the brass knob, the door slowly swung open by itself to reveal another truly astonishing sight.

The bedroom was set up similar to Amanda's, but the

furnishings were different. Barbara looked at the black and white sleeping quarters and gazed upon the bed where a little girl slept, but it wasn't Amanda. Barbara could easily and directly see that it was a completely different young female and there was an instantaneous resemblance that was noticed. She observed the young child as she stood beside her and the girl shifted, ever so slightly, and raised her little head to peer up at Mrs. Sterling. Barbara's heart began to race as she realized that the child in the bed was the same little girl who had brought her there—the same girl she stood beside in complete shock and disbelief. Barbara and the girl remained in the dark hallway, outside of the bedroom, and as the young anomaly pointed into the room, Barbara had an epiphany. She'd seen pictures and heard the stories. Her daughter had a friend who seem to reside in this room. Barbara herself had had more than one experience in there. The girl in the bed was Dortie! She was better known, though, as Dorothy Murphy. Barbara looked down again at the little girl and focused on her long blonde hair and her cute little dimples. In amazement, she realized that she could see the blue of Dorothy's eyes, in the otherwise colourless world, which clashed with the dark blackness of the rings underneath them. The frilly white nightgown she was wearing mimicked that of the sleeping girl in the bed.

    Barbara watched as a small ball of light appeared

next to the girl's bedside. She felt complete comfort and even refused to question where her own daughter was, as she came to the quick conclusion that she was not in her present state. The light in the bedroom quickly increased in size and moved, hovering just above Dorothy Murphy while she quietly and unwittingly slept. The astonishing energy shifted to the side of the bed, once again, and manifested into the shape of a large human male. Barbara squinted her eyes and tried to recognize the apparition, but the bright light it emitted was far too strong and brilliant to make any possible verification. The thick grey wool blanket that covered Dorothy slowly crept down the bed and fell off the end, exposing the little girl's body. The arms of the new anomaly reached down and seemed to penetrate Dorothy's face, moving right through her head and illuminating the pillows upon which she slept. As the bright stranger lifted his arms, the pillow slid out from under Dorothy's head, which gently dropped down onto the sheet and mattress ... but the girl didn't wake. Barbara gawked at the sight in front of her, then turned to look down at the girl beside her again. This time, the spiritual energy of the youngster showed an unpleasant expression of sadness and despair. Barbara looked back, just in time, to witness an all too frightening vision. She tried to speak and call out to the energy, but her mouth refused to open and she remained mute.

The intimidating force in the child's bedroom lowered the pillow gently onto the little girl's face. It seemed to lean in and apply a constant and damaging pressure. Barbara looked on in horror and promptly understood that the presence was essentially trying to suffocate the sleeping girl. Barbara tried once again to call out, but was unsuccessful. She wasn't even able to force tears out of her stressed eyes, although her emotions were flooded with discomfort and pain. The girl was awoken by her sudden inability to breathe. Her little body squirmed and her legs kicked in desperation. Her arms flailed and she attempted to remove the pillow from her face, but the powerful force decreased any real probability of that ever occurring. As Barbara continued to helplessly watch, the spirit beside her bowed her head to the ground. Soon the helpless little girl in the bed stopped her struggling and became motionless. Barbara could sense, almost immediately, that the girl was likely dead. She had been suffocated by the unknown force that surrounded her.

Traumatized by the horrific event, Barbara tried again to enter the room, but it was to no avail. She was stuck in place, as if her feet were enclosed in cement. The energy released its pressure on the pillow and faced the doorway. The shape of its head faced directly toward Barbara Sterling as it rose up above the little girl's unresponsive body, bringing the pillow with it. It seemed to hover three feet above the bed. All at once the pillow glided through the air and across the room, slamming into the little side table beside the closet, where it made solid and direct contact with a lit kerosene lantern. The gaseous flame landed hard on the ground and smoldered for a moment before sparking and igniting the lace cloth covering the table. Barbara watched in horror as the energy responsible decreased in size and reverted back to the shape of a basketball. The orb then moved toward the scared woman and girl, standing at the doorway, passing right through Barbara and causing her to inhale deeply, swallowing her fear. Her alarm was quickly replenished when Barbara rapidly turned her head to notice the bright ball of light head down the hallway behind her, disappearing into the washroom. She spun her head back just in time to see the closet door catch fire. A thick, acrid smoke began to fill the room and Barbara knew she could do nothing to assist the lifeless body of Dorothy Murphy. The bedroom door then gently closed as the fire inside intensified and Barbara opened her mouth once again to cry for help, but no sound escaped. As an old cuckoo clock in the hallway read 4:45 a.m, the master bedroom's door opened and a woman exited the room, followed by a large gentleman. Barbara could make out the facial features of the two adults and could tell that they were the same people she had seen in Donald's library photos. It was Marion Murphy and her infamous husband, Charles. They ran to the closed door and stood directly within Barbara and the accompanying child, who watched closely with an obvious sadness riddling her tiny face. She looked up to Barbara's gaze once more, telepathically relaying an instant message of education to the Sterling woman.

Barbara stood facing the door as Marion opened it and felt a sudden flood of energy rushing away from her as Charles announced he was going for water, after telling his wife to wait and to stay put. The bedroom released a suffocating smoke, but neither Barbara nor the spirit of Dorothy were affected. Marion peered into the bedroom after screaming her daughter's name and caught a glimpse of Dorothy's lifeless body on the bed, before covering up her face and rushing in to help. After a couple of minutes, the fire had spread up the walls and had broken the glass in the bedroom's window. As the frantic Murphy woman tended to her little girl, Barbara saw her tiny guide reach out her hand to her again. Barbara grasped her hand and electricity flowed through her body. The two of them began to move backwards, down the hall and away from the bedroom where the utter chaos was taking place. Barbara's feet flew out of her warm slippers and slid, uncontrollably, along the ground. It was at that moment that the little girl's bedroom door swung toward them and slammed shut again in a violent and aggressive fashion.

The spirit of Dorothy Murphy stopped in front of the open washroom door and Barbara moved up beside her. Feeling as though her feet were bolted to the ground again, Barbara peered inside the bathroom, where Charles Murphy filled a metal bucket with sink water. This was futile however, as the blaze that was burning inside of Dorothy's room was far too intense to be extinguished by the contents of the large, but ineffective container. Charles' body was shaking in apparent fear and a look of confusion and remorse was painted on his face.

Dorothy and Barbara watched closely as an anomalous, electric image suddenly appeared in the bathroom mirror. It was a male and his face was fear-provoking. His eyelids were peeled back, inside of his head, and his pupils were non-existent. The reflection's mouth drooped open and exposed black rivers of dried saliva that rolled down his cheeks, which were caved in with guilt. The man in the mirror showed himself as an independent image to that of Charles Murphy, and bared his yellow teeth while staring at Charles with the whites of his eyes. Barbara continued to watch attentively and witnessed Mr. Charles

Murphy, who appeared to be magically hypnotized, drop his half-full bucket of water, which landed on his lap and continued down, crashing to the floor.

Barbara could see the little girl beside her lower her head, afraid to view what was next. She could see that the smoke continued to billow out of the child's room. The last time her little friend lowered her head, the spirit of the man in the bedroom smothered the sleeping child with the pillow. Charles began to vibrate painfully and his right hand cramped up as it lowered to his waist, pulling up his shirt and exposing his .44 calibre pistol. Barbara took a deep breath and squinted her eyes. Charles took the loaded weapon out of his pants and looked straight at the terrifying image of the man in the mirror. He raised his arm and tilted the gun until it lined up with his temple. Barbara tried again to call out and move toward the man to stop him, but it was no use, and before she could prepare a clever, secondary plan, Charles Murphy had pulled the trigger, forcing his blood to splatter against the mirror where the mysterious reflection of the horrifying, distressed man precipitously disappeared. Barbara opened her mouth and tried to scream at the top of her lungs, but no sound resonated. As the creaky door to the washroom slowly closed shut, Barbara looked sideways at the little girl, who peered back at her with a look of extreme sadness on her face. Barbara could hear Marion, in the bedroom at the end of the hall, screaming for assistance, in pain and frightened. She closed her eyes and her head started to once again twirl inside, causing another mesmerizing sensation of euphoria and complete satisfaction. The spinning that was occurring in Barbara's head eventually subsided and the next thing she knew, she had returned to her present and familiar reality. Barbara cautiously opened her eyes wide. Her surrounding shone in amazing Technicolour, even in the early morning darkness.

After the cobwebs had removed themselves from her brain, Barbara shot around from her place in front of the bathroom door and looked for the little girl—the ghost of Dorothy Murphy. She wasn't there. She turned back to the washroom door and quickly opened it to peer inside. After flicking on the light switch, she could see that all seemed ordinary and that there was no indication of the traumatic experience she had just endured. Barbara's breathing accelerated and she snapped her head to the left, looking through the bathroom wall, as if it weren't there, and toward her daughter's room. She ran out of the bathroom, leaving the lights on, and darted down the hallway where she burst into Amanda's bedroom and turned on the light. Instantly, she observed her little girl, safe and still asleep, undisturbed by the recent events. The room showed no residual damage from any fire and the strange anomaly was gone. Barbara quietly walked over to Amanda's side and leaned down beside her.

"I saw Dortie tonight, my dear," she whispered. "You were so right. I'm sorry that I ever doubted you. I love you ... so much."

Amanda stirred slightly, but didn't wake up, and Barbara looked lovingly at her youngest child, watching her every breath. After two minutes or so, Barbara leaned over and kissed Amanda on her forehead twice before getting up to leave the room, turning off the light and gently closing the door.

She walked back down the hall and turned off the light in the bathroom, before peering toward the four occupied bedrooms. Then she walked back to the master bedroom, quietly pushing open the door and immediately noticed that the side lamp had been turned on. Donald Sterling sat upright in the bed and glared at his wife with a look of obvious disgust on his face. Barbara closed the bedroom door behind her and swivelled around to quickly address her husband, but as she began to shape her mouth to speak, she was interrupted before any words escaped.

"And how was that?" he asked. "Was that enjoyable for you? How about you fill me in with your enlightened and profound conclusions? Are you prepared to do that, Barb?"

Barbara was caught off guard by the questions. She

crossed her arms in front of her chest and assumed a defensive posture, fearing that her husband was not exactly who he professed to be.

"Did you see what you wanted to see?" he continued. "Are you happy now? I told you to leave it alone, didn't I? You just can't leave it alone, can you? Richard comes back and he's okay now and all you want to do is piss me off. Well, maybe it's time for someone to leave ... huh? What do you think about that? Maybe someone needs to get the hell out of here to make everything better." Barbara started to weep. "I'll tell you what, Barb," Donald poured on the guilt, "how about I leave now ... and you can sit here and figure out how you're going to leave later." Donald stormed past Barbara without making eye contact and attempted to leave the room. His arm was grabbed by his quick-acting wife.

Barbara looked Donald in the eyes and remembered the advice that Maria Prescott had given her— advice that was repeated by her son during their recent and meaningful talk. *Don't provoke him,* she thought. Don't provoke him. That was the most important thing to be remembered in order to keep the peace in the house ... at least until Maria Prescott came up with a plan to help. Her thoughts raced and she tried to think of a rapid plan to dissolve the animosity. She remembered what had worked, only six weeks prior, just before Richard had come home. Barbara smiled at Donald and flattened her right hand on his bare chest.

"I'm sorry, Donald, please forgive me." She stood on her tippy toes and whispered into her husband's ear. "Make love to me, Donald. Make love to me like you used to. I want you so much right now." She tilted her head sideways and brushed her lips against Donald's. After a momentary pause, Donald responded to his wife's sexual affection and passionately kissed her. He leaned over and lifted Barbara off of her feet, moving her to the bed where he proceeded to feverishly undress her and himself. For the next forty-five minutes, Donald executed like a rabid, wild animal, forcing Barbara to bite down hard on her arm and pillow in order to prevent the shrieks from their consensual satisfactions from leaving her mouth.

The outside temperature plunged and it began to snow. So much had been explained to Barbara Sterling, and now everything was beginning to make perfect sense. But she couldn't help but wonder if the evil one was not only present in their house, damaging her loving family and causing extreme pain and calamity, but perhaps also actually residing inside the body of the man who intimately shared her bed.

17
A Challenged Resolution

November 2, 1979

The Sterling family began to unravel. Although Richard was back home and doing very well, Donald and Barbara were becoming estranged from one another. They would still sleep together, but they were rarely intimate. The two steered clear of each other most of the time, passing in the hallways without much eye contact or communication. The children were all well aware of the tribulations within their household, but tended to side with their unhappy mother, who remained the most level-headed parent. The two girls were now afraid of their father and the volatile temper he possessed, and Richard avoided any confrontation with him. The Sterlings' dog, Misty, knew it also. She would often change direction when he approached and spent much of her time curled up on Mary's bed. Barbara's inspirational intuition flourished with her new writing project and she spent many hours in her office, when she wasn't tending to her children's needs. Money was no longer a desperate issue for the Sterlings. Even though Donald was hardly ever working, the windfall found under the bulky oak tree in the backyard, along with Barbara's recent book having reached bestselling status, seemed to put the family's monetary woes behind them, for now.

It was a Friday afternoon and the three children had just returned home on the bus from school, ready to start their weekend. Barbara typed away in her office and Donald sat in the living room, staring blankly at the powered-off television while sitting in the armchair. He wore a collared, striped button-up shirt, with his sleeves rolled halfway up his arms. Lately, the family had noticed that the inside of Donald's forearms were developing long and painful-looking markings, which were (more than likely) caused by his own doing. The presumed scratches were crimson red, deep, and looked quite uncomfortable, but no one else in the family, by this time, was at all interested in helping or offering any him any sort of medical attention to comfort his physical ailments.

Richard and his two sisters laughed and roughhoused at the bottom of the stairs. They took turns chasing each other around in a small circle and tagging one another while they whacked at each other's back sides. Richard ran behind Amanda and grabbed her around the waist, lifting her off of the ground and making her scream with delight.

"Come on, Dee-Dee, now you try and lift me up. That will be a neat trick."

Mary laughed and began making an irritating robot-like noise with her voice. The exuberant activity climaxed to a crescendo, which drew a reaction from Donald.

"That's enough," he stated sharply, "Be quiet now!"

The three Sterling children purposely disregarded their father's request for silence and continued with their childish sibling bonding. Amanda screamed while Mary made electronic beeping noises and Richard attempted to actually speak over top of everyone else, with his loud and dominant deeper voice. Donald turned sharply toward the staircase and prepared his second attempt to quell the infuriating racket.

"Quiet, God Dammit! Didn't you hear me?" His voice escalated. "Stop with the bloody noise! You are all driving me nuts!"

The kids calmed down for a moment and stared at their frustrated father. Amanda went back almost immediately, after an inconvenient break, to wrapping her arms around her brother's waistline in a futile attempt to lift him off of the ground.

"Chill out, Dad, we're just fooling around," Richard said. "No one is fighting. We're just having a good time." He returned his attention to his sisters and the decibel-level amplified once more. Donald then stood up from the chair and made his presence well known. He took a step around the seat and stumbled toward his children; anger riddled his face.

"ENOUGH! You sons of bitches! I told you ... stop your fucking noise!"

Donald growled and hissed as he doubled the amount of breaths he was taking. Mary and Amanda, frightened by Donald's anger, scurried down the hall toward their mother's office, and Richard stood tall against the base of the bottom stair, bravely looking his father straight in the eyes.

Donald hesitated, as if contemplating his next move, then burst toward Richard with his fists clenched.

"Maybe you need your ass kicked! Is that it boy?"

Richard turned quickly to run up the stairs, fearing his dad's next move. Donald followed closely behind, stalking his son like a wild predator moving in for the kill. Just past the midway point of the staircase, Donald reached out to grab Richard's blue v-neck shirt, and a voice cut through the chaos, penetrating the thick air in commanding fashion.

"JIMMY, STOP!"

The brash female's voice acted as a stun gun, stopping both Sterling males in their tracks and preventing the imminent clash.

Richard took great advantage of his father's hesitation and finished his journey to the top of the wooden stairs, while Donald slowly twisted his rigid body around to face the source of the inconvenient interruption. Barbara had come out of her office and now stood at the end of the back hall with her girls cowering behind her. She stared over at the intruder who had halted the dire situation. It was Maria Prescott. She had returned and entered the house from the front door without invitation. Donald took a step back down the staircase, and addressed the stranger.

"What did you just say?" he asked.

"I told you to stop, Jimmy." The woman stood, owning her space, and wearing an exact replica of her last outfit, except that this one was a dark, menacing shade of red. "I think that you heard me now, didn't you?"

Donald came down two more steps, coming closer to Mrs. Prescott's massive form.

"Who the hell are you?" he fumed. "You must be

mistaken, lady. My name isn't Jimmy."

Barbara spread out her long arms to shield her young girls, still standing behind her, and the concern on her face shot through the room as she waited, patiently, for some sort of confrontation to break the tension. She opened her mouth to speak, but was cut off immediately by the woman she had met only two months prior.

"Oh, but of course you are," Maria confirmed. "You *are* Jimmy … and you know it to be quite true … don't you, Jimmy?"

"I don't know what in the hell you're talking about, lady!" His voice became disdainful and annoyed. Barbara moved to a closer vantage point near the bottom of the stairs, to better observe her husband. Her son, Richard, remained frozen at the top. "You shouldn't be here, you crazy bitch. Maybe you should be in hell … Maybe, I'll take you there!"

Donald rushed down the remaining four steps and lurched toward Maria Prescott, grabbing her around her thick neck with both of his hands and driving her backwards, where they both slammed hard up against the wall, beside the front entrance. The medium let out a gasp and a painful squelch as her body hit the wall. Barbara took a few steps toward them and started screaming commands at Donald.

"Donald, stop! Stop it right now! What are you

doing? Oh my God, Donald, please don't do this!"

Misty, reacting to the commotion, ran from the office to the living room, bypassing the girls and her adult mistress, heading toward the infuriated man, and barking hysterically. Donald tightened his grip around Mrs. Prescott's neck and ground his teeth. The look on his face represented an irate and entirely uncompassionate human being who was willing to inflict as much damage as possible.

"This will teach you to break into someone's house, you crazy bitch! Maybe now you'll learn your lesson!"

Barbara continued to plead with her husband, who ignored her presence and bore down on the stranger's throat. Misty continued barking at Donald's thigh and Amanda and Mary screamed in the background, holding each other tightly. Donald looked down at the yapping golden retriever and bared his bottom teeth, which he paired with an ominous grin. While choking out the helpless woman, he swung his right leg back and trust it forward into the dog's belly. Misty yelped and rolled away from the scene with commanding force. She quickly jumped up and soon realized that her body's injuries would certainly prevent her from re-confronting her master. She hobbled away, to the horror of the other family members, and retreated to the confines of the kitchen, out of everyone's sight. Donald showed no remorse and drowned out the cries from his loved ones as they screamed and pleaded for him to stop what he was doing. His attention soon reverted back to the enormous woman. He seemed determined to finish the job quickly.

Richard, who had started to bolt down the stairs when his dog was assaulted, instinctively ran toward his father with a determined and steadfast adrenaline rush. He leaped forward with his outstretched arms and landed on his father's back, putting him into a tight full Nelson and applying pressure to ensure that he wouldn't lose his grip.

Donald finally released his grasp on Mrs. Prescott's neck and turned slightly, as the weight of his son buckled his legs. He reached up around his head to grab the teenage boy, who was not about to be tortured in the same manner. This time it was Richard's turn to bare down, shifting his entire body weight toward the floor. He turned sharply and threw his father down, hard. Their bodies created a loud thud when they made contact with the hardwood, and Donald lost his wind for a brief moment. The Sterling family and Maria Prescott were surprised and astonished by Richard's heroic actions.

"Leave her alone," he thundered down at his stunned father. "You can't do that to people … are you crazy?" He pointed at Donald, who shook his head and slowly stood up to face his son. Mrs. Prescott coughed and clenched her neck muscles in an attempt to gain some air. Her bulging eyes were surrounded in dark rings and her skin looked a shade of pale blue. Amanda and Mary, by this time, had raced around the back hallway and through the dining room to meet their injured dog, who lay under the dinner table. Barbara let out a shout and was paralysed by the current events involving her loving, but conflicted family.

Comfortably back on his feet, Donald darted his eyes back and forth around the room. He looked at his wife, his imposing 17-year-old son, and an innocent but viciously violated and assaulted stranger. He was surrounded. An intense intimidation developed within his soul. After taking a long look at Richard, Donald turned and slowly retreated to the basement, where he slammed the door behind him. Barbara ran to Maria's side to console her as she struggled to oxygenate herself. Richard gave his mother a big hug and was overcome by emotion, so he limped away and headed upstairs to lie down on his bed.

The two exhausted women walked arm in arm to the chesterfield in the living room. Barbara instructed Mary, who came in to report on Misty's condition, to get their unexpected guest a tall, cold glass of water from the kitchen's tap. Mary brought in the thirst-quenching beverage and handed the glass to Mrs. Prescott. She stared closely at the woman and prayed that she would make everything better.

"Thank you so very much, my sweet child," she said in appreciation. "Please, let me talk to your mother alone for a moment, my dear."

Mary glanced to her mother, who nodded slightly, and Mary began to leave.

"Mary, honey ... how is our Misty girl?" Barbara feared the worst in her response.

"I think she's going to be okay, Mom. Amanda is using a bag of frozen peas on her chest. I told her she had to do that, because I think Misty is bruised there. I don't think Dad meant to do it, Mom." Mary looked over once more at Mrs. Prescott and left the room, going back to the kitchen to help her little sister with their dog's painful injury. After completely regaining her wits and breathing capabilities, Maria Prescott focused her attention on Barbara's dejected eyes and finally levelled with her, once and for all.

"Barbara, the evil one is here. The evil one is inside of your husband ... but it's *not* your husband Barbara. It's not Donald inside of that man's body at the moment. And it's not Charles Murphy either, Barbara. It's someone who is much more dangerous, and he's the one who hurt your son as well."

"I don't understand; who are you talking about? Who, exactly, is allegedly possessing my poor husband?" Barbara looked defeated. "You *are* trying to tell me that my husband and my son have been possessed ... is that right?"

"It's the spirit of Jimmy Murphy, Barbara. The teenage son of the Murphy family, who took his own life back in 1937." She glanced toward the side door. "On the tree in the corner of your backyard. He hung himself to spite his own father and succumbed to his guilt. The evil one is Jimmy Murphy, Barbara. He lives in a different realm than the others. A different realm than us."

Barbara wiped the tears from her face and looked at the ceiling.

"Is there anything we can do? Will there ever be any hope for our family, Mrs. Prescott? I wouldn't even think straight if I lost someone I loved. I can't even imagine what I would do, or how I would react. Please help us, Mrs. Prescott! Tell me that there will be no more loss."

"Yes, Barbara. Yes, I will help you! I'm here to help you and save your family from the evil presence of this Jimmy Murphy." Maria paused for a brief moment and continued. "Barbara, did your son happen to visit you when he was in the hospital? In his spirit form?"

Barbara looked up and couldn't believe what the medium was asking. How could she have possibly known that something as unbelievable as that had occurred?

"Why yes ... yes he did. It was the day we got the call that he had come out of his coma. He said that everything was going to be okay. I remember because I couldn't move or speak. Well, *we* couldn't move or speak, that is. He was younger. Like when he was about 10 years old or so. It was a euphoric moment for me. I thought we had lost him, but somehow he was all right—"

"Barbara," Maria cut her story short, "did he tell you anything else?

Barbara thought about the series of events, then answered the mysterious woman.

"Yes ... he said, 'Dig the tree, Daddy.' I remember him telling us that, if Donald dug the tree, everything was going to be all right." She squinted her eyes and thought about her next words. "Donald dug up the money from under the tree. He found a lot of money there and it really helped us out during a rough time."

Maria hastily interjected, "Jimmy Murphy committed a malevolent crime, Barbara. He stole a tremendous amount of monetary funds from his parents in 1936—funds willed to them by his own grand folks. Jimmy took those funds and placed them in an old chest that belonged to his grandfather. Then he dragged the chest outside, into the backyard, where he dug a hole and buried it beneath that intimidating oak tree. He was pierced with guilt, Barbara. His conscience plagued him ... and after a confrontation with his father in 1937, Jimmy took his life in the very same tree ... but Barbara, I'm not referring to the money. The spirit of Richard that you saw that night was telling your husband to dig *the tree*. Not *beside* the tree, Barbara. To dig the tree itself; don't you see?" Puzzled, Barbara looked at Maria, and Mrs. Prescott continued. "The tree contains an important link. It's a residual haunting that you are witnessing and it is directly connected to the death of Jimmy Murphy. He made a choice and now he rebels in spite of the consequences."

"You're not suggesting that Jimmy Murphy became a malicious spirit because he took his own life, are you Mrs. Prescott?" Barbara felt tears welling up as she thought of old friends, and her very own uncle, who had also taken their own lives out of desperation and fear for their futures.

"No Barbara! Jimmy chose to take his own life and it was a tragic and saddening time, but these spirits are at peace most of the time. Jimmy's suicide is not punishable on the other side. It is because of his crime, which he was not held accountable for, that he was damned to the evil side—the realm of darkness, if you will. He was given no choice."

"Please tell me more, Mrs. Prescott." Barbara began to understand the series of events.

"He has been holding the others prisoner, Barbara.

He has caused an accident and kept the spirits of the rest his family locked down here, in a completely different realm. The Murphy family, Barbara … they have been trying to warn you this entire time. Trying to save you from Jimmy."

Barbara stood up from the couch and stepped toward the fireplace, turning her head toward Maria.

"The Murphy family … how do we set them free, Mrs. Prescott? How can we help them escape their pains and bring them some peace?"

"*We* don't do anything," she explained vigorously. "*You* won't do anything, because you are unable to set them free, otherwise you would have done it by now, am I correct?" Barbara felt compelled to nod in agreement. "Therefore," Maria continued, "*I* will be the one who will set them free. That is why I am here. I can do this, but you cannot. Understand?"

"Yes … yes, I think I do understand. Oh, it would be so appreciated if you could do that for us. Tell me then … how will *you* do it Mrs. Prescott? How will you set them free? Is this something that you've done before?"

Maria struggled to get up from the chesterfield and moved to Barbara's side, standing near the fireplace.

"Well now, that's a good question." She leaned in and whispered into the Sterling woman's ear. "I can't set the Murphy family free until we remove the spiritual energy of Jimmy … and yes, as a matter of fact, I have done this before."

"Okay, and how are you going to achieve that Mrs. Prescott?" Barbara looked insensitively into the round woman's stare. "How are you going to remove the spirit of Jimmy Murphy?"

"Well *I* can't," Maria admitted, "but I know someone who most definitely can."

18
Release, Rejoice, Re-evaluate

November 2, 1979

By 5:30 in the afternoon, the skies outside darkened and a thick sleet began to pelt the outside of the Sterlings' house. Maria Prescott was strolling around the interior, smudging the cracks in the doorways and the panes of the windows with a dragon's blood sage. The distinct scent soon filled the room and Maria knew she had to work fast before Donald came up from the basement. Barbara was asked to protect the children. They managed to help Misty upstairs, and they gathered in the master bedroom.

Maria stayed downstairs, and stood in the centre

of the living room with her head bowed. She clasped her hands together and began to mutter to herself. Her words were inaudible but appeared to form some sort of bizarre prayer. The house became instantly cold. The ceiling light in the living room swayed back and forth and a gentle humming filled the air. Maria spoke aloud.

"Jack? Jack Mobley. I need your help now Jack. You owe me remember? We had a good talk the other night, now didn't we, Jack?" She turned and faced the fireplace, continuing to speak out loud to the empty room. "I told you that you were trapped in the evil realm. As a result of that alleged murder, remember Jack?" Maria looked to the ceiling and continued addressing the spirit of Jack Mobley, the convicted killer who had been accused of murdering a young boy in the basement of the very same house almost eighteen years ago.

"I believe you, Jack ... like I told you just the other night. I know that you weren't responsible for taking that young boy's life. We agreed on that, remember? We agreed that the boy scribbled the initials *J.M.* in the bloody mess with his finger before he died, didn't we? Because he was made to do so by his killer, who knew you shared those initials and would be implicated. Because he was compelled to gloat about it, signing what he had done! We know who the real killer was, don't we, Jack?" Upstairs, the master bedroom door opened and Barbara crept out to get a better look at the woman's actions. "Only you can help me, Jack. Only you can send Jimmy Murphy away. Only one who shares the evil realm can dispose of an evil entity. I need you now Jack ... please."

A familiar, heavy clomping sound resonated from behind the basement door. It was Donald Sterling. He was coming up and Maria Prescott was not yet ready. She had failed to summon the assistance from Jack Mobley, and now she was alone in the direct path of a disgruntled psychopath who had already tried to kill her once.

Donald threw open the basement door, which slammed against the wall from the force of his thrust, and walked briskly into the living room's entranceway. He immediately cowered in disgust at the aroma of sage that permeated the air. The house began to shake, as if a small earthquake was occurring. Maria didn't back down and stood her ground in front of a still fuming Donald, who pointed his finger at the unwanted stranger.

"Okay lady, you asked for it. It's time for you to go." Donald began advancing toward the medium as an imposing sound penetrated the living-room area and stalled Donald's progress. A bright sphere of light appeared about four feet off the ground, expanding in size until it resembled a full grown man, his body fading to nothing below his waist, his legs (if they were there) invisible. The amazing manifestation hovered between Donald and Mrs. Prescott, facing the heavy-set woman, who straightened the glasses on her face, adjusted her sleeves, and smiled.

"Hello Jack. Thank you so much for coming."

Donald stood frozen with fear, no longer displaying his aggressive persona. He couldn't. It was clear that he was no longer the dominating force within the room. Barbara remained at the top of the stairs and watched the events that were transpiring below her in awe.

Maria Prescott knew, all too well, that Jack was making a tremendous sacrifice, as his interference with this subject could result in his spirit also being released into the evil afterlife—the cold, insignificant, nothingness that awaited evil spirits who ultimately crossed over to their final destination.

"Jack, it was Jimmy Murphy who caused your eventual incarceration. It was he who finished your life and caused you to die a lonely and unsuccessful man. He is in the body of the man behind you. He's in his mind. Take him, Jack. Take him with you and free this family from their tortures. Make him pay for ruining your life, Jack. Revenge is sweet."

The apparition of Jack Mobley spun in the air, turning and facing Donald with a blank expression, the light being emitted from his powerful energy pulsating throughout the angry house, which continued to quiver and shake gently. The spirit of Jack raised his arms and reached out to Donald. His arms extended in length, inching closer and closer like seeping gasoline.

"You don't have any power here!" Donald yelled at the anomaly, and then he turned to Mrs. Prescott. "Neither of you have any power here! You've made me very angry, God dammit! I don't know what you think you know or why you accuse me of these things! You don't have any power here; do you hear me?"

He was disregarded. Donald felt that he needed to escape before he was fully consumed by the aggressive dynamism that surrounded him. He looked franticly back toward the basement door, and at that moment, it slammed shut, even more violently than when Donald had opened it minutes earlier. Fear coursed through Donald—fear of a loss of control.

As the frozen rain continued to unleash a constant pounding on the rooftop and sides of the house, Mrs. Prescott looked up to the top of the staircase, made eye contact with Barbara, and smiled with delight. By now the children had joined their mother outside of the master bedroom. They were terrified and weary, but the Sterling family could finally sense the tense and ultimate conclusion approaching. Sorrow swept through Barbara and she felt as if she were losing her husband, once and for all. She stood helpless as the apparition of Jack Mobley gradually floated toward Donald, showing absolutely no remorse.

The colossal apparition of Jack Mobley encroached on the Sterling patriarch and pinned him up against the wall beside the basement door. Its light intensified, and in one gentle effort, it fully enveloped Donald's cowering body, which immediately became stiff and rigid. Mrs. Prescott let out a commanding cackle as Mary and Amanda screamed in fear from the top of the staircase. Barbara couldn't stop herself and bolted down the stairs, instinctively rushing to her husband's side. Before her arrival, and during a severe reprimand from Maria, Donald clenched his eyes tightly and opened his mouth wide. His glasses shook off of his face and crashed down to the ground, and his body began to shudder in waves. Barbara stopped in her place at the bottom of the stairs and lifted her hands, shielding her eyes from the intense brightness that surrounded her husband and projected from inside of him.

"What's happening?" Barbara screamed in horror at Maria. "Make it stop! Make it stop, *please!*"

"It's just about over, Barbara," the medium said. "Soon everything will be the same as it was before you and your family came here to Clover Springs! Donald needs you Barbara! He needs you more than he's ever needed anything before! You have to be supportive now! Nothing else matters. You must fight for you husband."

Controlled by a concealed and unmistakably commanding force, Donald began to rise, levitating just off of the ground, and moving slowly toward the front door of the house. Donald threw back his head and let out a chilling scream, causing his son and two daughters, on the upper floor, to beg for his release. He continued forward, his solid body reaching the door and pressing relentlessly into it. Maria promptly waddled herself forward toward Donald's helpless form.

"Come Barbara! He needs you now!" Mrs. Prescott and Barbara arrived behind her man's radiant body and reached out to grab his thin t-shirt and the waistband of his pants respectively. Donald's body continued crushing against the closed door, which creaked and showed signs of structural failure. Maria turned to meet Barbara's eyes. Richard, who told his sisters to stay put, scrambled down the staircase to assist his frightened mother, his father, and the obviously angelic stranger.

"Pull!" screamed Maria Prescott. "Pull and bring him back from the evil side. Pull with everything that is inside of you." The three of them clamped down on Donald's garments and shoulders. They braced themselves and closed their eyes, pulling hard against his body, which acted like the rope in a cruel game of tug of war. As their combined strength began to overpower the forward momentum of Donald Sterlings' body, it separated from the thick wooden door, creating a dark and ominous void.

"Keep pulling, Barbara! Don't stop, whatever you do. Don't stop pulling!"

As the momentum shifted, a flowing grayish mist emerged from Donald's chest. It heaved away from his frame and flattened against the door, creating a swirling black wall of smoke. Barbara, Richard, and Maria found new reservoirs of strength and Donald's clothing began to rip and tear in their grasp. All at once, the four of them were flung to the floor, as Donald's body was suddenly released from the commanding energy, which continued on through the front door and outside into the elements. The house became unusually quiet and stopped shaking immediately. Mary and Amanda stayed put, as they were told, and remained silent, attempting to hold back their obvious terror.

Richard was the first to get up. He ran to his mother, who was lying on the floor a few feet away, and grabbed her hand to help her to her feet. The two of them embraced lovingly and ran to Mrs. Prescott, who was struggling to regain her feet. The three of them looked down the hall to where Donald's limp body lay motionless and awkwardly twisted. Barbara cautiously approached him and knelt at his side, turning him over onto his back.

"Oh my God." Barbara started to cry. "He's dead!" She looked over at Maria. "He's dead, isn't he Mrs. Prescott? He's dead! We've lost him, haven't we?"

"No Barbara," Maria said. "No. He's not dead. I know he's not dead, because I don't sense his energy any longer. The evil energy is now gone and his peaceful energy remains here in a living state. He's not dead, Barbara. He has endured a truly traumatic experience, and you saved his life!" She looked over to Richard. "You both saved him. Jimmy Murphy is gone! Jack took him away to the evil ending place. He won't be back." She paused, lowering her eyes. "Neither of them will be." She was saddened by her thoughts of Jack.

Donald stirred, and after an anxious moment or two, opened his eyes. His wife was crouched over him. His eyes welled up with tears and a slight smile crossed his lips. Richard handed Barbara his father's glasses and she placed them back on his face, pushing them tightly against him. Donald licked his lips and reached up, slowly grabbing his wife's arm.

"Hi Barb. How are you?" Donald spoke softly and was clearly a much different person than the one they had come to expect. Barbara wept and leaned over to hug her long-absent man. "I was so worried about you," he said. "I don't know what I would do if you weren't okay, Barbara."

She held him even closer. "Hi sweetheart," she

answered, chuckling at the absurdity of the moment. "I'm fine. How are *you*? That's the question. Do you feel all right?" She pulled back and looked at him.

"I feel really good, Barb. I feel free ... I don't think that he's in me anymore. I love you so much, honey, and I'm so sorry for being such a royal pain in the ass. I honestly can't believe you stuck it out and didn't just leave me here to rot and die."

"It's okay; you don't need to apologize, Donald. This wasn't your doing." She looked over to Richard and up to her girls, who were slowly making their way down the staircase to connect with the rest of their family. "We understand it all now, honey. We know that you didn't intend to hurt us. We know now, and it's going to be okay."

Maria Prescott looked up the staircase. The girls were about halfway down. "STOP!" The two girls came to an immediate halt. "They are all free now, and they want to leave," Maria explained. "Don't move girls, because they are ready to leave *now*."

Donald, Barbara, Richard, Mary, and Amanda Sterling, along with Maria Prescott, stared up to the top of the staircase at a truly amazing sight. There, hovering well above the top stair, were three distinct light anomalies. As they manifested as human forms, something spectacular took place. The apparitions expanded, developing legs and feet. As the bright lights shone, the two Sterling daughters were afraid to move. They stayed where they were, halfway up the staircase, and held tightly onto the banister. The brilliance of their light dimmed somewhat when the three entities finally revealed their true selves. It was the Murphy family. Marion, little Dorothy, and Charles Murphy. They stood side by side at the top of the stairs, expressionless and spookily translucent. The three points of concentrated energy began walking down the staircase, all abreast and in unison. Dorothy took each stair with a noticeable limp, dragging her left leg behind her. She wore the same white nightgown that Barbara had seen earlier during the little girl's tour of events. As the three full-bodied apparitions met up with the girls on the midway point of the staircase, they passed right through them and out the other side. Dorothy Murphy turned her illuminated head, and her eyes, still surrounded with dark circles, darted toward Amanda Sterling. She lifted her arm and spread out the fingers on her hand, appearing to smile slightly.

"Bye-bye Dortie." Amanda lifted her right arm and waved at her ghostly little friend. "I'm going to miss you, Dortie. I hope you can be happy now with your mommy and daddy."

Dorothy slowly turned her small head back to the front and the three spectres continued down the staircase to the bottom, where they proceeded forward, stopping suddenly and directly in front of the chesterfield. The three Murphy spirits looked to the right, directly at Donald, Barbara, and Richard Sterling, communicating their obvious gratitude with their eyes. After about ten seconds, the softly glowing figures passed through the large picture window, out to the front porch, and slowly disappeared into the dark and violent elements.

The house felt warm and inviting for the first time in recent memory. Donald made his way back to his feet and hugged Richard tightly, assuring him that he was in a safer place now. Mrs. Prescott shuffled her way over to Barbara and placed her arm around her waist.

"It's over, Barbara. I told you I would fix this for you."

"Yes, thank you Mrs. Prescott. You have no idea how much this really means to me. How much this really means to my whole family. How can we ever begin to repay you?" Barbara's extreme happiness finally exploded and she hurled her arms around Maria in stark appreciation. The great and clearly self-confident medium reciprocated Barbara's embrace and then straightened her arms to push Barbara back to a less invasive position.

"Barbara, the intelligent and evil energy that existed in your house is now gone." The rest of the family listened to Maria speak. "There will be residual energy that remains. Don't be afraid, Barbara. The residual energy can't hurt you. I will make arrangements to remove the big oak tree in your back yard. That will help you a little bit. But don't be afraid; the residual energy is harmless." She took one last look around. "Well then, I think that my job here is done; don't you think?" She walked to the front door, crammed her feet into her winter boots, and threw on her enormous coat, which she had hung up when she arrived. As she opened the door, she turned back around and finished answering Barbara's final question while adjusting her bosom.

"My bill will be in the mail, Barbara. Well then ... until we meet again." And with that, Maria Prescott took her leave.

Barbara reached out and grabbed Donald around his waist, embracing with him again, as the children gathered all around to rejoice. Donald was fine. He was present and normal, loving and quite accountable. It appeared as if the Sterlings' fortunes had finally changed for the better, after nearly three gruelling and unfortunately long years. The news could only be positive from this day forward ... clearly.

19
Should Auld Acquaintance Be Forgot

December 24, 1979

Christmas Eve had finally arrived and it was much to the joyous anticipation of the Sterling clan. The family was whole and all paranormal activity, as promised, had stopped. Even the residual activity that the medium had warned about was not evident. The big oak tree in the backyard had been removed. A Contracted tree removal company had showed up the previous Wednesday and topped it before cutting it down right to the abundant, broad stump, which remained a prominent reminder of the past. This just so happened to also be the same day that Donald, after some long debate with the entire family, put their house up on the open market. It was decided that the memories of the home, over the last three years, would not be healthy for their souls, moving forward—even though they had been to Doctor Snyder for private, individual diagnoses and all passed successfully.

Donald was whole once again, a loving, supportive role model to his children and a solid pillar of strength for his beautiful wife, Barbara. He easily remembered most of the incidents during his ordeal: from the verbal assault on his wife to the physical assault of Mrs. Prescott and his own dog. He could remember the monster that he had become and vowed to make amends to those who he had hurt. The rest of the family trusted this to be genuine and celebrated the fact that their loving father had returned to them with no long term, adverse effects.

The family sat around the Christmas tree, shortly after supper, to reminisce. Misty was by their side, having fully healed from some sore ribs, even forgiving Donald's actions and approaching him often with a wagging tail. They planned to take a walk, later in the evening, to view the lights adorning the houses up and down their block. This was a special time for a healing household.

Richard was also back to his usual self, his unnaturally white hair notwithstanding. He had learned a very valuable lesson from his taxing experiences with the Murphy family: He would never take things for granted ever again. He would appreciate the things he had and find a comfort in the people who were in his life—who cherished and loved him the very most. Even his home education, which had become surprisingly trivial and simplistic, had quickly accelerated to the point where the Sterling family decided to re-enroll him in school earlier than anticipated. Richard would still graduate from high school at the end of May, even after missing two years of his vital education while in his coma. It was cause for great celebration.

The family members listened to carols on their record player, which Donald had borrowed from Mary's room. They all toasted with a cup of hot apple cider and took turns announcing what they were most thankful for, as a new year was on the horizon and it was also the end of the decade.

The first to take her turn was 8-year-old Amanda, who proudly sat upon a large cushion beside the blazing fireplace.

"I am most thankful for my daddy," she stated. "I thank that he is not mean to us anymore and wants to play with me more again." She smiled and looked around the room for approval. Donald gleamed and affectionately reached over to stroke her long brown hair while holding back tears.

Amanda's involvements with the Murphy family were extremely frightening, but they didn't seem to cause any extended lingering psychological trauma. It was basically concluded that Amanda had lived, symbiotically with the spirit of Dorothy Murphy. They shared the same bed, played with the same old dollies, and it was quite possible that little Amanda Sterling had many more encounters with the ghostly Murphy girl than were ever reported to her parents or siblings. Full-blown conversations with little Dorothy would have surely become a common place event for Amanda and her tiny, active, developing brain.

Next to give thanks was the middle child, Mary. She was developing into a beautiful young lady, now 14 years of age, and her courage and fortitude exuded moxie with each of her movements.

"Ummm, well let's see. I would say that I am the most thankful for having Richard back. I was really scared when you were sick and I didn't know what I was going to do without you if you died. Thank you for being so strong, brother. I love my whole family … and even Misty too. I love you too girl." Mary caressed the dog from her chair beside the enormous pine, which had been decorated with popcorn strings and bright shiny balls.

Looking back, Mary knew she had been quite lucky during her time with the Murphy family, and Jimmy

Murphy, in particular. She was thrust down the stairs and was lucky that she was not injured more severely. Being the middle child and a female made her less of a target for the evil Murphy spirit. The room that Mary occupied had been vacant while Jimmy, Charles, and Marion lived there, and remained unoccupied after his death and the introduction of Dorothy. Although very much perceptive, Mary would be the very least likely to experience the Murphys' haunting in an intelligent or residual sense.

Barbara seemed to be just a touch uncomfortable, and even nauseated, as she invited Richard to take his turn. The now 17-year-old miracle child sat on the love-seat, which he and Donald had turned toward the festive tree and the warmth of the crackling fireplace.

"Well, this is an easy one for me," he said. "By far, I am most thankful for my life, all of yours, and the escape of the others. The experiences that I had when I was asleep were ones that I will never forget … that I can't ever forget. I got to see you at your lowest and I got to see those who were already gone and they were at a point much, much worse." The family looked deep into Richard's eyes as he continued. "I saw what it was like to be on the other side and it wasn't very nice, but everybody kept telling me that there was a better place. A better place than here even. But no one is able to report from the final destination … no one knows ... no one ever will until they arrive ... and by that time, there will be nothing left to report on. Yeah ... it's the experiences that I had when I was fast asleep that I am most thankful for I think ... because I knew that those experiences would bring me back to all of you." Barbara leaned over and gave Richard a colossal hug, but still appeared green and unsettled.

Richard Sterling was extremely fortunate to be alive. He immediately became a scapegoat to Jimmy Murphy as he was the closest to Jimmy's age. A young male who stayed in the same room that his energy resided in, he was a defiant, but easy target for possession. And not a demonic one requiring an exorcism, but a vindictive, selfishly motivated and controlling one. This was caused by Jimmy's life choices and his ultimate punishment from the other side for severing his lifespan far too early, before he could atone. The remainder of his actions were the unfortunate choices made by his spiritual being. Richard's sickness and poor attitude were directly caused by the spiritual energy of Jimmy Murphy, who lived inside of his body and ate away at his soul. This is almost exactly what happened to Donald Sterling as well during his unravelling ordeal.

Events that had taken place over the past three years had aged Donald prematurely. His face held lines that hadn't even existed prior to their relocation to the

Murphy house. But there was a happiness that wasn't apparent before too, just skin deep, and this added vibrant colour to his cheeks.

"Well, this is easy for me, also." He scanned his adoring family. "I am most thankful for you … my children, and my soul mate, my beautiful wife." He paused and glanced at Barbara, who had managed a sincere smile, but still looked nauseated. "The Sterlings are fighters! We don't quit and we can overcome all of our adversities. Nothing can stand in our way!" He reached up and pushed his glasses tighter to his face. "I guess there is a lot to be thankful for, huh? I think that I'll drink to that." He tipped back his mug of apple cider and swilled the warm contents while his family members joined in on the toast. It most certainly hadn't looked as though they would ever celebrate as one solid family unit again, and Donald was going to guarantee that he took full advantage of his second chance.

Once the evil spirit of the infamous Jimmy Murphy had caused Richard to be hospitalized and slip into a coma, it vindictively moved on to plague Donald Sterling. It was a continual vendetta, which stemmed from an unfortunate disagreement with his own father, which had led Jimmy to target the males of the Sterling family while holding his own father, Charles, captive on the other side. Donald was aware of his circumstances, but unable to clearly communicate what he felt inside. Even when the energy was travelling outside of his body, Donald was helpless and remained an inmate, just like the rest of the Murphy family. By all accounts, Donald Sterling had been a puppet.

The ultimate positive outcome would be for them all to finally leave the *"freak show,"* once and for all, relieving the entire family of the memories lurking around each and every corner.

"It's your turn, my dearest." Donald looked to Barbara, and he and the children awaited her answer.

Barbara smiled and opened her mouth slightly, as her breathing rate increased and her head began to spin.

"There are so many ..." She quickly closed her mouth and held her breath. The rest of the family looked at her, mortified.

"What's the matter with you, Mom?" Mary asked, "Are you all right?"

"You don't look very good, Mom," Richard perceptively added. "I can go get you some water if you want me to."

Barbara placed her hand over her mouth and jumped up, racing to the downstairs bathroom. The family listened as she vomited, while the holiday classic, "Mary's Boy Child," played in the background. Little Amanda stood up and took a step toward her mother's location.

"Daddy, what's the matter with Mommy?" Amanda was confused by her mother's ill timing. "How come Mommy is so sick in the bathroom, Daddy? Maybe Mommy needs some aspirin or Vicks Vapo rubbed on her chest."

"I'm not sure Dee-Dee; she doesn't feel good. Maybe she has the flu or something. I'll give her a minute and go check on her if she isn't back."

Mary, who had jogged down the hall to listen closer at the bathroom door, came running back into the living room.

"Yeah, she's puking all right. It sounds like a lot of puke too. I can hear it landing in the toilet and there's a lot."

"Gross!" Richard gave Mary a playful push on the top of her head. "Okay, we get it Mary, thanks for the visual. It's just what I needed."

Mrs. Sterling had been a solid rock through the paranormal happenings caused by the Murphy family. She experienced the voice of Dorothy, from within Amanda's room, and even her own son, in a younger body, floating above her and waking her from a deep sleep, not to mention the creepy vision of Marion Murphy and the truly unfortunate discovery in the basement. Barbara had a gift and seemed to attract the energy from the afterlife. It was quite evident, though, that Mrs. Barbara Sterling was the super glue that held the entire family unit together, through the good and the bad times.

Barbara returned after cleaning herself up. She was drinking water from a plastic cup that she had kept in the downstairs washroom. She looked a little bit better than she had only minutes before, but it was apparent that she was still fighting with her immune system.

"Are you all right, Mommy?" Amanda asked. "Mary said that you were puking and we think it's a little bit gross. Do you have the flu, Mommy? Santa is coming tomorrow you know. It's a bad time to have the flu."

"I'm fine honey. I'm just a little tired, that's all. Well, shall we get ready for our little walk?" Mary and Amanda nodded. "Rich, can you get Misty's leash for me. It's in the kitchen, on top of the fridge I think." She was displaying a heroic front, but still didn't look too well. Richard nodded to his mother, and Misty, sensing that a stroll with her family was in the works, followed behind him into the kitchen. Barbara smiled at Donald, who recognized that there was something that she wasn't telling him.

After locking the side door, the Sterling family walked down the driveway and into the night, toward the street and brightly lit houses of celebration. A light snow fell and covered the more than twenty spruce, elm, and oak trees that surrounded the Sterlings' property. The family walked in a close group with Misty leading the way, pulling Barbara behind her. About halfway down the driveway, Amanda turned around and looked back toward their gloomy, faintly lit house. Something had caught her eye. Everyone continued to walk, but Amanda stopped, seeing a man sitting on the porch. Even with the limited visibility, the man seemed solid and obvious. He stared blankly through the trees of the front yard and slowly lifted his head to look up into the sky.

Amanda quickly turned around to announce the man on the front porch, so that the rest of the family could see, but her mother commanded everybody's attention as she had started vomiting again. This time, all over the driveway, and it splattered onto Richard's tan rubber boots. Amanda rapidly turned her head, once again, toward the porch, but the man that she had clearly seen was no longer there. She immediately turned back to her mother. Her father, brother, and older sister were surrounding Barbara, consoling her in her apparent discomfort and gently pulling the hair away from her soiled mouth. Helping her stand back up straight, Donald used his thumb to wipe some of the saliva from around his wife's pouty lips. He wrapped his arms around her and then pulled away.

"You're getting sick a lot, Barb," Donald stated. "This seems to be so sudden. It's not a very Merry Christmas for you this year, now is it? Let's go back to the house and maybe you could lie down for a while."

Barbara stood up straight, weaving for a moment as she commanded her balance, before wiping her face with the sleeve of her brown suede overcoat.

"I have something that I need to confess." She managed a devilish grin, which intrigued all of her loved ones. "I was really hoping to save this announcement until we all woke up tomorrow, because it was supposed to be a Christmas gift for everyone, but I guess that I better explain myself, because I don't want you all to be concerned."

Richard and the two girls were perplexed. They stared at their mother with squinted eyes and patiently awaited her news. Donald's mouth opened in awe, as he had an instant epiphany, and wrapped his right arm around his wife's shoulder to show her the loving support she needed to continue on.

"I'm pregnant." She forced an enormous smile through her nauseated disposition. "I got the call yesterday from Doctor Snyder. He said that when he examined me, he saw some signs and ran tests for it. I'm about eight weeks along already. We're going to have another baby in the house guys. A new brother or sister for you kids. A beautiful, new human being with sincere innocence, who hasn't been polluted by our recent trials and tribulations. I'm so very excited for all of us. Merry Christmas everyone!"

20
Update

July 17, 1980

In May of 1980, the Sterling family left the two-story home on the corner and moved to a newer neighbourhood on the other side of the ever-growing township of Clover Springs. The renowned Murphy/Sterling house and property, once again, was possessed by the town. Donald finally handed over the keys to the lot commission for a financial loss, after unsuccessfully trying to sell the house before their desired time frame. Word of the tragic events that had recently taken place, in and around the cursed house, were kept surprisingly private and shielded from the gossiping women and townsmen. It was rumoured that the town of Clover Springs had plans to finally follow through with their initial plan, from 1944, to convert the property into a large family park—a large family park less one humongous oak tree in the far back corner. For now though, the house would be boarded up and the furniture covered over once again.

A locked gate would be added to the huge iron fence and a landscaper would be hired to maintain the grounds until the town's plans came to fruition.

Barbara Sterling was extremely expectant now. It was a complete miracle that she had nearly made it to term, as there had been a number of challenging hurdles along the way, many more than with her previous three pregnancies. She had been in and out of the clinic several times and Doctor Snyder had made more than a few emergency house calls over the last eight months. Unfortunately, she'd spent much of her challenging second trimester suffering from a troublesome indigestion that caused her a number of horrible nightmares while she slept. The day of expectancy was only three more weeks away. Barbara and Donald were thrilled to welcome a new member to the family, but Barbara was cautious. Something was out of place and didn't seem quite right.

Soon, Amanda Sterling would no longer be the baby of the family, and Richard would eventually be moving out on his own, to take some secondary schooling and pursue a career in engineering. Mary had developed into a lovely young lady, who became a spitting image of her mother and a joy to her loving father. It was refreshing and fortunate that no one in the family had lasting effects from their haunting at the old house. Even Misty displayed a confident attitude within her new surroundings. The *"freak show"* was no longer occupied and soon it would cease to exist at all. But the memories would last indefinitely.

Barbara sat in the chair at her new office desk. A huge picture window gave her a view, over her typewriter, of a rolling, blooming meadow across the yard, spanning three acres at the edge of town. The new house was only possessed by serenity. Barbara had been struggling with her pregnancy, but spent every free moment writing. Her latest project had transformed into a memoir, and she felt that it would develop into her crowning achievement. Her greatest triumph to date. It was her first non-fiction work and it consumed her time while waiting for child number four to joyfully arrive. As she worked on the last paragraph of the final chapter of her manuscript, Barbara paused and looked up, staring through the window at the blazing afternoon sun. Then she continued and typed her last few words. She sat back and cringed, laying her hand upon her swollen belly and stroking it from top to bottom. Quite satisfied with her progress, she ripped the last page from the typewriter and placed it, upside down, on the thick pile of existing papers. She took her thumbs and carefully slid them under the pile, flipping it over and exposing the title page. After tapping the more than three hundred pages on her desk to even out the paper, she laid the pile down and admired it, smiling from ear to ear.

With little warning, Barbara buckled over and grasped her belly with both arms. Writhing in pain, she called out to her family, in need of immediate assistance.

"Help me! Please, something is wrong. Help!"

Donald was the first to hear Barbara's pleading and quickly entered the well-lit room, where he saw his wife doubled over in her office chair.

"Oh my God, Barbara, what's happened to you? Are you all right?" Richard, Mary, and Amanda also heard their mother's calls and ran to be by her side.

"Something is wrong, Donald. It's too early. I think that something is really wrong. I need to get to the hospital and I think it should be right away." She ground her teeth and rocked in pain. Donald grabbed his wife under her arms and lifted her toward his body.

"Rich, call an ambulance!" He helped his wife walk and they headed out of the new office. "Come on, honey. Let's go and have a quick lie down on the chesterfield until the ambulance arrives. Just take some nice long breaths, honey; everything is going to be just fine ... I know it."

"I'm so sorry, Donald. I was hoping that you wouldn't all have to fuss over me like this." Barbara hobbled to the chesterfield and lay down. "I'm so scared, Donald. What if something is wrong? I don't think that I could handle even more setbacks. That wouldn't even be possible now, could it? After everything that we've been through?"

"You're going to be just fine, honey ... I'm right here and I'm not going anywhere. You are the strongest person that I know. Just lie still and the ambulance will be here soon."

As Mary followed her parents out of the office, the cuff of her green blouse caught the top page of Barbara's most recent manuscript, flipping it into the air. There it floated, back and forth, until gravity brought it to rest on the floor beside her office chair. It was the title page of Barbara's most recent work and she had perceptively entitled it, *The Pale Murphys*.

Acknowledgements

I am so greatly thankful to the following people for their inspirational submissions to this project. Each one of their depictions contained a genuine level of believability and, in result, compelled me to fictionalize the experiences which assisted in bonding the final storyline of *The Pale Murphys*.

Kathelin Francis — For your fascinating story about the female spirit who motivated you to follow her into your son's bedroom where he was in need of assistance. Perhaps a guardian angel? Your story enticed me to depict your experience in chapter 6 of *The Pale Murphys*. Thank you for your contribution.

Carrie Giesenger — For your emotional experience and vision of your mother after she had just passed. The reference to her in a younger body inspired the storyline in chapter 10 of *The Pale Murphys*. Your connection to your loved ones is strong and endearing. Thank you.

Becki Henderson — For your truly amazing, out of body, experience involving your mother. Your inspirational story is recognised in chapter 10 of *The Pale Murphys*. Thank you for sharing your unique and captivating memory.

Also Mike Blackwell and the University of Saskatchewan — Your "ghost" story, based on real events, was easily altered to produce one of the creepiest experiences in *The Pale Murphys*. The finding of Richard in chapter 6. Thank you Dad, for sharing your story.

About the Author

Steven Blackwell has a strong connection to the paranormal, having experienced numerous events. Between the years of 1994 and 2004, while living with his wife and two young children in a townhouse in Campbell River, B.C., approximately a dozen undeniable paranormal happenings fully sparked his interest in the subject, inspiring his first book, *232 Birch*—a real-life memoir relating to those experiences.

Dabbling in paranormal investigation over the past four years, Blackwell and his wife have been privileged to investigate the Bird Cage Theatre in Tombstone Arizona—considered to be one of the most haunted locations in North America—on two separate occasions.

"Many people are intrigued by the paranormal and its mystery. I believe that science is getting closer to answering the questions that skeptics often ask. If you've experienced something in your life that you can't quite explain... You've had a paranormal experience." — S. Blackwell

The Pale Murphys, although fictional, contains adaptations of actual experiences from accounts collected from Blackwells' family and friends.

Printed in Canada